A CAPTIVE *in* WILLIAMSBURG

PETER REESE DOYLE

DRUMS *of* WAR

Volume 3 in a Series

Providence Foundation

A Captive in Williamsburg

Published by:
The Providence Foundation
P.O. Box 6759
Charlottesville, VA 22906
(804) 978-4535
provfdn@aol.com
www.providencefoundation.com

Cover illustration:
Corky Nell

The Providence Foundation is a Christian educational organization whose purpose is to assist in the development of liberty, justice, and prosperity among the nations by teaching and equipping people in a Biblical philosophy of life. The Foundation teaches Christian principles of government and politics, economics and business, arts and sciences, education and family life, using historical models which illustrate their application.

Printed in the United States of America

ISBN 1-887456-13-9

A Captive in Williamsburg

Peter Reese Doyle

TABLE OF CONTENTS

To

DR. PETER WOODBURY WESTON

Whose Delight is in the Law of the Lord

Virginia
December, 1775

John Murray, Lord of Dunmore, had devised a Brilliant
Plan

To crush Virginia's Freedom: He'd attack by Sea and
Land!

His Ships would block her Coastal Trade, and strike the
Coastal Towns;

He'd hire the Indian Tribes out West to rally and come
down

Upon the Patriot Settlements with Bow and Spear and Fire,

While Redcoats marched with Tories armed 'gainst those
who dared conspire

To 'scape Great Britain's Rule and Might, Her recent
Claim to Power

Unchecked by Law or Ancient Rights!—Her brutal drive to
tower

Above her Constitution, Albion's own Fair Liberties

That long protected Englishmen from Kings' Brutalities.

For England's King and Parliament had brushed off Ancient Law

And meant to crush the Liberties and Freedoms that they
saw

Free Englishmen across the Sea had 'stablished in this
Land,

In every Colony they'd built with their own Blood and
Hands.

But Patriots in the Colonies did not intend to fall

Once more into Dread Slavery! They rallied at the Call

To take up Arms and fight for what they'd earned by their
own Toil,
So greatly blessed by God Himself—rich Seas, and fertile
Soil,
And Liberty—with Godly Laws! And Legislators picked
By their own Choice, bound fast by Law, Who could be
quickly plucked
From Office if they reached too far beyond their lawful
Bounds,
Dismissed when their brief Time expired, While better
Men were found.

Lord Dunmore meant to crush the Patriot Forces by his
Plan;
He sent his Soldiers inland, confident that—Man to Man—
His Redcoats were superior to Patriot Volunteers,
And would most surely quell Militia Units should they dare
To face the British Volleys, stand firm 'gainst British Steel,
And foolishly attempt to halt the turn of History's Wheel,
Which had just seen Great Britain humble European Foes,
Destroy their Armies, one by one, and send their Ships
below
The thunder-stricken Deep, till every Nation now had
owned:
"Brittania rules—The Sea! The land!—Her Might the
World has Crowned!"

CHAPTER ONE

The Chase

Low-flying scattered clouds raced repeatedly across the face of the moon. Even when these passed, patches of light just barely filtered through the tall trees to the rough dirt road that wound through the forest. The rider knew that he'd never be able to see deadly potholes before his horse stepped in one— and broke an ankle. Andrew rode his horse at a slow trot, praying that the British patrols had not yet gone so far inland as to intercept him.

The stallion was nervous; that he could tell, and it required an iron grip on the reins to keep him in check. And if there was barely light enough sometimes to see the road, there was certainly not enough for him to be able see any riders waiting in ambush in the darkness ahead, nor in the thick, black, menacing shadows on either side of the narrow, twisting pathway through the tall trees.

The packet of messages the Patriot scout had given Andrew was tucked securely in the left-hand holster in front of the saddle. A pistol was stuffed in the other saddle-holster, and Andrew's long rifle rode in its deerskin scabbard in front of his right leg. In his belt the boy carried tomahawk and long knife. Andrew knew that the British had been warned about the Patriot messengers. He knew also that he dared not put the horse into a run as long as he was in this dark forest. *I can't take a chance on Dusty breaking his leg in a pothole!* he realized.

Until he was out of the forest, he'd not be able to ride any faster.

Yet speed, the messenger had told him, was essential!

Andrew's mind flashed back to his meeting with the Patriot scout half an hour before. "Just take these messages to the boat," the rider had told him. "Bill Holland's waiting there with his crew; he'll get the letters to the militia units!"

"Is it urgent, sir?" Andrew had asked.

"That it is, boy!" the scout had answered soberly. "Governor Dunmore's troops are making another raid on the plantations along the river. They attack by sea, wherever they wish, and do their robbing and plundering without hindrance, before our men can gather to oppose 'em. We never receive warning in time. But tonight our spies in the Governor's camp tipped us off. And if we can get the news to our mounted militia, they can ambush the British when they land, and stop 'em from destroying another plantation and looting its arms and stores!"

"But you have to hurry!" the scout added.

Andrew wanted to hurry. But he knew that at least another mile separated him and the stallion from the end of the tall trees. He dared not put the horse into a gallop until he got out of the dark forest and could see the road ahead.

Another mile at this slow trot! Andrew thought to himself, casting his eyes desperately to left and right, seeking to pierce the impenetrable darkness that brooded with silent menace on either side. *If British patrols stop me here, I'll be trapped for sure!*

"HALT!" a rough voice shouted suddenly from the darkness ahead. There was a tremendous crashing in the forest as mounted men burst from the trees on either side of the road and blocked his way!

Instinctively, without thought, Andrew drove his heels into *Dusty's* sides and yelled into his ear. The big stallion leaped ahead, smashing into a large white horse directly before him, knocking the animal down and throwing its uniformed rider to the ground. Slamming into another horse, Andrew's *Dusty* broke through the surprised riders and leaped away with increasing speed.

"STOP!" another voice shouted. The sound of a pistol firing exploded behind the fleeing stallion as Andrew bent low over Dusty's neck.

Another shot was fired, then another, but none found its mark in that dreadfully poor light. The big stallion bore Andrew swiftly through the dimly lit path that now made a sudden curve to the right.

I'm out of sight! Andrew realized as he rounded the curve. His heart pounded wildly in his chest.

He was out of sight—temporarily—but not out of danger! There were yells behind him, angry shouts, and Andrew knew without doubt that the mounted patrol would be in instant pursuit.

But I can't slow down! he thought, as he bent low over the galloping stallion's neck, praying that no unseen branch would sweep him out of the saddle, no unseen pothole would break *Dusty's* leg and bring them both crashing to the ground. Desperately the big steed pounded through the narrow path between the trees.

Behind them now, the British lieutenant who'd been thrown to the ground was scrambling back into the saddle. Roaring his rage and humiliation, the officer wheeled his big horse, then kicked spurs into the animal's sides. As the horse leaped in pursuit of Andrew, the lieutenant reached into the holster in front of his knee. He drew out a long pistol, cocked the weapon, and shouted that he'd kill the fugitive who'd knocked him down in front of his own men.

"He's a rebel messenger, all right!" he shouted. "We've got to capture him or he'll warn the Patriots of our raid!"

The half-dozen mounted men behind him kicked spurs into their mounts and pounded after the lieutenant. They too had pistols in their hands, and they too knew that they had failed in their mission to intercept the Patriot messenger. They had better not fail again—they *had* to capture him! The men who'd already fired stuffed their empty weapons into saddle holsters, and reached for their other pistols.

They'd been so sure! They'd gathered in two bunches, one on either side of the road, just inside the trees, waiting for the rebel to appear. They'd known that he would—their spy had told them of the rebel scouts along the river. And they'd known that if the Virginia militiamen were warned in advance just where the British raiders were going to land, they would swarm like flies gathered round honey, and ambush them along the shore!

And the British patrol's plan had worked! They *had* trapped the Patriot messenger!

But to their shock and surprise and shame, the rider had burst through their trap and galloped away!

That man was too fast! the lieutenant swore to himself as he spurred his huge horse to greater speed. *We had him boxed— who would have thought that he'd break through seven mounted men and ride me down?* Stung with shame, his spirit boiling with outrage at the indignity of being unhorsed in front of his men, the proud officer shouted vengeance as he galloped through the darkness. He kicked his splendid horse into a reckless pace and gradually pulled ahead of his men.

Bending low over their saddles, the galloping men behind him spurred their horses in the desperate chase through the poorly lit passageway through the forest. One false step, one hoof put into an unseen pothole, and a horse would break its leg and plummet with its rider to the ground. But there was no help to it! They could not slow down—they had to capture that man ahead! They could not let him get away with news of the coming British raid!

A bare hundred yards ahead of the furious pursuit, Andrew came to the fork in the road that he had passed several hours before. He'd planned to stay on the road as it bore to the left. This was the broader way, the way from which he'd come. From that road he could in another mile turn right and take the narrow path that led to the river and the waiting boat.

But they'll expect me to stay on the road! he realized. Instantly he made up his mind. *I'll take the right fork. They can't know about the boat! And this fork takes me to the river as well.*

Andrew swerved the horse onto the right-hand fork, and galloped down the curving path that was suddenly thrown into even greater darkness as a passing cloud concealed the moon.

They'll not see me change direction! he thought to himself with sudden hope.

But the outraged British Lieutenant was riding a powerful horse, and he'd drawn closer to the fleeing boy than Andrew had realized. The officer was able to get a brief glimpse of the stallion ahead just as its rider turned onto the fork that led into the trees.

"He's going right!" the lieutenant shouted to the men behind, as he too turned onto the right-hand fork in pursuit of the fleeing Rebel messenger.

But the galloping horsemen behind him never heard the Lieutenant's words over the pounding of their horses' hooves! Nor could they see him behind the bend in the road when he made the turn to the narrow path. Knowing that the larger road led more directly toward the territory controlled by the Patriots, they assumed that the Rebel rider would head straight for his own troops. The reckoned also that their lieutenant had taken that way too. When they rounded the curve they kept on the main road and pounded on, spurring their horses to greater speed when the moon came out for a moment behind the clouds and threw a bit of light on their way.

The lieutenant didn't know that his men had remained on the main road, and that he was now alone!

Pounding through the darkness, Andrew realized now that he *had* to slow down! This path was too narrow, the light too dim, the footing too treacherous for him to let the big stallion continue this mad gallop through the treacherous forest. The boy pulled back on the reins and forced the animal to slow his desperate pace to a rapid trot. Even this, he realized, was madness in such all-encompassing darkness—he could barely make out the path between the trees!

Within two hundred yards a large clearing burst suddenly into view. Andrew trotted *Dusty* into this clearing, searching fearfully for the path on the other side. But just at that moment a patch of clouds swept across the face of the moon! The darkness became almost impenetrable, and he pulled the animal to a sudden halt. He had not had time nor light to find the way out! Turning to his left, he searched the darkness ahead for signs of the path that led to the river.

The stallion stumbled suddenly over a fallen tree, and went down! Andrew leaped clear just in time, as the horse fell to the ground, rolled over with a frightened whinny, scrambled to his feet and trotted across the clearing, far out of Andrew's reach!

The moon appeared just as quickly as it had disappeared, bathing the clearing in silver light. As Andrew leaped to his feet he heard the galloping rider behind him.

The British lieutenant burst out of the forest and spotted Andrew at once. Yelling with mad delight at the sight of his quarry unhorsed, the officer fired his pistol as he yanked his mount to the left, and rode toward Andrew.

But the ball passed over the boy's head. The officer dropped the pistol from his hand and drew the large cavalry sabre from its scabbard on his side. Shouting triumphantly, he spurred the big horse toward Andrew, knowing now that he'd caught the fleeing messenger and could cut him down with one blow!

Andrew's guns were on the horse—and the horse was trotting away across the clearing, utterly out of his reach! Whirling to face his pursuer, Andrew whipped the tomahawk from his belt, waited until the rider was almost upon him, threw with all his power and skill and leaped to the side as the big cavalry-horse thundered by.

The tomahawk whirled over in its deadly flight and buried itself in the Lieutenant's upper chest, knocking him out of the saddle to crash sprawling on the ground as the animal galloped past. Andrew drew his long knife and raced toward the fallen officer.

But the man lay still, flat on his back with his arms outstretched, moaning and breathing hoarsely. The long sabre had fallen some yards away. Andrew knelt beside the stricken man, yanked his tomahawk free, then turned and sought his horse.

The stallion had come to a halt at the far edge of the clearing. Meanwhile, the British officer's horse had veered to the left, away from the stallion and close to the trees. Then he'd trotted back toward the path from whence he'd come. He found the narrow opening in the woods, and disappeared from Andrew's sight.

I've got to catch Dusty! Andrew knew. Else he'd be caught afoot by the rest of the British patrol. Slowly he moved toward the skittish stallion at the far side of the clearing, speaking softly, calling him. The animal moved away, very nervous still.

Andrew knew his plight was desperate.

Those other soldiers will burst out of the woods any minute! I've got to get that horse!

Slowly he walked across the clearing, speaking softly, praying that the animal would let him come close. The stallion snorted nervously and trotted thirty yards away. Andrew halted again, and fought to control his growing panic. *I can't scare him!* he realized. He continued to speak quietly to the frightened animal. Then, once again, he began to walk slowly forward.

Dusty let him approach—then moved away again! But he didn't go as far away as he had before.

He's got to be scared in this forest! Andrew thought. Again the boy waited a minute; then he moved forward again.

Speaking slowly, softly, Andrew moved with infinite patience. Again the stallion snorted—but he didn't move away! Finally, Andrew came to the animal's side. Carefully he reached for the reins and gripped them in his fist. Yet he waited another minute, speaking quietly to calm the nervous beast. Finally, he stepped into the stirrup and swung into the saddle. The animal snorted and bucked half-heartedly, then quieted. Andrew turned his head, and searched for the path that led to the river.

There it is! Just barely visible in the wall of trees, that narrow opening *had* to be the path! Andrew trotted *Dusty* forward. The stallion moved willingly—but with a limp, Andrew realized suddenly.

Half an hour later, Andrew rode up to the landing where he saw several men standing. Behind them in the river he could make out the outlines of a small boat.

"HALT!" a sentry challenged.

Andrew halted the horse, and identified himself. "I'm looking for Mr. Holland," he said.

"Here, son," a big man replied. "I'm William Holland."

Andrew leaned from the saddle and handed Holland the package. "From Lieutenant Johnson's patrol, sir," he said. "The British are mounting another raid on the river plantations, and Lieutenant Johnson's asking for mounted militiamen to ride fast and stop them. This letter tells where they're heading and how many boats they have."

"Thanks, boy," Holland replied, whirling and leaping into the small craft beside the dock. The two men with him scrambled quickly into the boat, threw off the lines, and sat to the oars.

"Pull, men!" Holland said. "Then we'll set the sail! We've got to get upriver!"

"Thanks, son!" he called again, as the skiff swept swiftly into the river and began to disappear into the darkness! "Don't let the Redcoats or Tories catch you!"

Andrew turned the stallion, and took the trail that led to the road that would take him toward Williamsburg. The path would parallel the river for a while, he knew, then head inland.

"I've got to watch for those other riders!" he reminded himself.

He pulled the long-barreled pistol from its holster and rode into the darkness. The stallion was limping still. Andrew prayed that the other British riders would not find him with an injured horse.

"I'd never get away from them if they caught up with me now!" he realized.

Meanwhile, the six British soldiers who'd stayed on the main road had galloped madly for over a mile before slowing down. But the sergeant had realized finally that they should have seen the lieutenant on the long straight stretch they'd been on for the last quarter mile.

"Where'd he go?" he shouted to the rider galloping beside him.

But no one could tell him. He yelled for the patrol to pull to a halt. With difficulty the men reined in their excited horses and milled around in the road.

"The lieutenant must have taken the other fork back there!" the sergeant cried out. "Hurry! We've got to go back!"

The men whirled their horses and dashed back down the road. When they came to the fork, they turned and took it. Soon after, they came to the Lieutenant's horse standing in the path ahead. The sergeant gathered the animal's reins in his hand, and led the group in a trot along the path. Not long after, they burst into the clearing and found their lieutenant sitting on the ground, hand clutched to his chest, holding his thick white neckcloth to stop the bleeding from his wound.

The men rushed to their officer and leaped to the ground. Carefully they helped the wounded man to his feet, then onto his horse. The lieutenant reeled in the saddle, but kept his seat. Slowly, the patrol walked their horses back the way they had come.

"I failed, Sergeant!" the lieutenant moaned bitterly through clenched teeth. "That Rebel got away!"

CHAPTER TWO

Ambushed

Hours later, just before the breaking of the cold November dawn, fifty mounted men filed silently through the forest toward the river. A hundred yards from the water, the men dismounted and tethered their horses to nearby trees. Leaving half-a-dozen men to guard the animals, the group moved stealthily along the narrow path to the water's edge until they reached the boat landing.

"Spread out, men," the captain said quietly. "Spread out on both sides of the dock. Stay back in the trees. Don't fire 'til I command!"

"Will you wake up the family first?" his lieutenant asked, as the men spread through the trees above the river bank.

"No," the captain replied. "Someone's liable to give the British warning. There's no way of knowing who's to be trusted nowadays!"

"At least we got here before the British did!" the lieutenant observed, as the two men stood in the dark shadows. Already the light of approaching dawn was touching the river; soon they'd be able to see the boats.

"Let's hope our information's correct," the captain replied. "Usually the British strike the plantations without warning."

Suddenly a militiaman loomed in the darkness beside them. "Captain," he whispered, "we hear the boats!"

"Back to your post!" the captain ordered at once. "Tell the men not to talk—you know how sound carries over the water. Wait for my order to fire!"

The lieutenant went instantly to the left of the line, warning the crouching men to wait for orders to shoot.

Now all the Patriot militiamen could hear the sound of approaching boats. And now the barest trace of light was creeping across the water. Suddenly, three sails appeared; beneath these, the militiamen could barely make out the dim outlines of ships' boats.

"That's a cutter in the lead," the captain whispered quietly to the militiaman crouching beside him. "It'll have a cannon on the bow, loaded with musket balls. Tell a dozen men to fire at the men around that gun first." Quickly these orders were passed to the men on either side, and the message went along the lines of waiting men.

Then the cutter's sail came down; at this signal, the sails of the other boats dropped at once, and the three craft coasted silently to the dock. The cutter landed to the left, the other two boats came to rest on the right of the long pier, and as they did so, men leaped out of the boats and threw lines around the posts to make the boats fast. At once, soldiers began to clamber out of the boats and onto the dock, their musket barrels gleaming in the faint light.

"Fire!" the militia captain shouted, aiming his own rifle at the dim figures crowded on the dock.

The air was shattered by a ragged volley as the hidden marksmen fired into the crowded formation of men pouring onto the dock from the three small boats. Cries of pain and alarm rose from the shattered group of men as the deadly shot struck them down. Men fell, some into the river, as others fired back at the rifle-flashes along the river's bank.

The boom of a swivel gun from the bow of the cutter exploded, and a cloud of musket balls swept through the dark toward the line of crouching militiamen. But the gun's crew had been cut down by the Patriot volley; the man who aimed the cannon was rushed, and the deadly lead balls ploughed into the ground below the bank behind which the men were firing.

Already militiamen were reloading, and firing as fast as they could. British troops fired back from the three craft as their officers yelled frantically for the men to jump back into the boats and push into the river. Struggling soldiers wrestled half-a-dozen wounded men aboard as the sailors shoved off from the dock. Some men rowed while others struggled to raise the sails of their stricken craft. Lights flashed from the musket barrels along the sides of the boats as the disorganized soldiers fired back erratically and ineffectively at the muzzle flashes from the hidden militiamen on the shore.

Birds were screaming in the forest along the river as the militiamen on the bank exchanged fire with the soldiers in the boats. Another swivel gun boomed, sending a cloud of shot into the trees. Slowly the boats pulled away from the dock as the sailors leaned to their oars. Then the wind caught the sails, and the boats turned, presenting their sides to the riflemen on shore, thus enabling more of their soldiers to fire at their ambushers.

But as the distance to the boats increased, the muskets of the soldiers were no match for the long range rifles of the Patriots. The soldiers continued to take hits from the deadly marksmen, falling back into their craft.

"Cease firing!" the captain called finally. "They're getting out of range."

A few more shots followed his command; then the firing ceased. From the cutter, the swivel gun boomed again. But the distance was too great for accuracy, and the musket balls ploughed into the dock.

"Lieutenant," the captain called, "send two men to warn the house. Tell them we beat the British off."

Then the captain called for his men to reassemble. In the growing light, the grins of the men were evident. "We got 'em this time!" one of them told the captain.

"That we did, Seth," the captain replied. "Finally, someone warned us in time to ambush those raiders!"

"Maybe that'll stop Governor Dunmore's raids on the river plantations," another said.

"I doubt it," the captain replied. "The Governor intends to retake Virginia. It hurt his pride to flee from his palace in Williamsburg, and he's determined to come back. If the British government sends him enough soldiers, he'll do it too. In the meantime, he'll keep up these raids. He's got a batch of ships, small warships and armed merchantmen. He can strike wherever he wishes, and we won't often be warned in time to stop him."

"He's got the advantage, all right" the lieutenant agreed bitterly. "Usually, we don't know when or where he's coming until it's too late."

"Well, thanks to our spy, and that messenger, we knew he was coming this morning," the captain said grimly. "He lost some men, too. That'll at least make 'em a bit cautious before they hit our peoples' homes again!"

"Any of our men hit?" the captain asked.

"Yes, sir. Two men. But no bones were broken, and they can ride."

"Thank the Lord!"

"The British left six men dead on the dock," a militiaman called out.

"And we wounded and killed more in the boats," the lieutenant added.

"Collect their muskets," the captain ordered briskly. "Let's stop at the house, and warn them to keep scouts down river, in case Dunmore plans to avenge this defeat. Back to the horses, men! You did a great job!"

Later that afternoon the tired company rode into their camp in Williamsburg. The two wounded men were taken to Doctor Galt at his Apothecary Shop on Duke of Gloucester Street, while the others went gratefully home. The captain and his lieutenant reported to the Patriot leaders. Soon the news spread through the town that Dunmore's raiders had been ambushed before they could loot another plantation.

Several hours before the militiamen returned, Andrew had been roused from a deep sleep. He'd come home while it was still dark, had tumbled exhausted into bed, and slept soundly since. Now, his mother shook his shoulder until he opened his eyes.

"I was dreaming!" he said. "A British patrol was chasing me and my horse couldn't move! Wow! I'm glad you woke me up!"

"Andrew, I hated to wake you," she said with a smile. "But your father wants you to meet him and Mr. Wythe and Captain Innes at Shield's Tavern. He wants you to tell them about your ride."

A short while later, Andrew dismounted in front of Shield's Tavern and tied the horse's reins to the rail. He paused, as he often did when passing the building, and looked at the curious brick smokestack that served the middle and right-hand section of the tavern. Then he mounted the steps and went in. Making his way through a cluster of men in the hall, he went to a back room and found his father deep in conversation with three other men.

"Sit down, Andrew," William Hendricks said as his son entered the room. "You know these men."

Andrew knew them all: Captain Innes, one of the militia leaders of the town; Mr. George Wythe, the distinguished lawyer and professor at the College of William and Mary, and Matthew Anderson. Anderson, though older, was a close friend, a frontiersman who had trained Andrew and his friend Nathan in Indian fighting. He was also the man who'd introduced him to the great Patrick Henry.

The men greeted Andrew warmly. Mr. Wythe was the first to speak. "So you're the messenger who brought the news to our militia in time to stop Governor Dunmore's raiders!" he said with a smile.

"Yes, sir," Andrew replied, awed in the presence of this gentle and brilliant colonial leader.

"Hear you had a tussle with a British patrol on the way," Matthew Anderson said, with a twinkle in his eye.

"Yes, sir," Andrew said, "they ambushed me."

"How'd you get away?" Captain Innes asked, puffing on his long white pipe. It was he who had asked the other men to meet in this tavern, rather than in the more oft-used Raleigh. "We can avoid the Governor's sympathizers better here, I think," he'd said.

The men listened intently as Andrew described the ambush, the chase, and the fight with the British officer. His father sat back in silence, trying without success to keep his face impassive and conceal the pride he felt in his son. He'd heard the story from Andrew earlier that morning when the boy had returned home, but learned more now as the three other men questioned Andrew closely about his adventure.

When Andrew finished, George Wythe looked at Matthew Anderson. "That's the first time we've been able to stop the Governor's raiders before he wrecked one of the river plantations! How did we get the news before the soldiers struck? You've been working with our scouts, haven't you Matthew?"

"That I have, Mr. Wythe," the woodsman replied, "but we usually don't get warned in time. This time, a man in the Governor's camp passed the information to our scout. He told us where the British were headed, and when they'd arrive. The scout got the message to Andrew here, who was waiting with another of our men, and Andrew managed to fight his way through a British patrol and get the news to William Holland. Holland had a boat ready, and he sailed back during the night to warn some mounted militia. He reached them just in time for them to ride fast and set up the ambush."

Captain Innes looked soberly at the others. "Gentlemen, if the British Government comes to its senses, and reinforces Governor Dunmore, Virginia will be in a bad way. Our militia units aren't yet ready—not like the Massachusetts and New Hampshire and New Jersey troops—and we're just not organized to stop a real invasion."

"Governor Dunmore's begged the British Government to send ships to blockade our coast, and troops to take our towns," said George Wythe. "And you're right, Captain, Virginia is not yet ready to repel a serious British attack."

"True, Mr. Wythe," Captain Innes replied, "but so far the Governor's only been reinforced by sixty troopers from the British Fourteenth Regiment that's stationed in Florida. Their commander's not releasing men until he gets reinforced himself. And the Governor sent his family back on his biggest ship, the *Magdalen*, so the small ships he's got can't establish a real blockade of our coasts. Not yet, at least."

"But the warships *Otter* and *King's Fisher*, and the armed merchantmen *William* and *Eilbeck* are doing a lot of damage!" Matthew Anderson said grimly. "They've caught some of our fishing boats and taken their catch. And they've caught some other boats with cargo from Britain and the West Indies. If the British Navy sends Dunmore more ships and men, Virginia's situation will be grave indeed."

"What about the Indians in the West?" Captain Innes asked. "We hear that Governor Dunmore's agent John Connollay is working among 'em. If Dunmore can set the Indian tribes against us, Virginia will be fighting for her life on her Western boundary and on the Atlantic coast as well."

George Wythe replied with a puzzled frown on his face. "You're quite right, Captain. But our agent to the tribes reported to the House of Burgesses that Connollay was not trying to raise the Indians against our people. And yet. . ." Wythe paused, choosing his words with care. The others waited. Then he continued: "But some of us are skeptical about that report. We know that Governor Dunmore will do everything he can to destroy Virginia and re-establish British rule; we think Connollay's working quietly to stir up the tribes to war against us."

"Daniel Morgan and Hugh Stephenson led their riflemen to Boston as soon as General Washington's plea for reinforcements reached Virginia," Captain Innes said. "Some fifteen-hundred marksmen are on the heights around Boston now. Morgan put his men on horses and covered six hundred miles in twenty-one days, without losing a man on the way! That's an incredible feat. Which is good for General Washington—but not so good for Virginia if Governor Dunmore succeeds in inciting the Indian tribes to attack our western settlements."

"You're right," Matthew Anderson replied. "That took away a powerful fighting force which we would really need to defend those farms and villages."

"That's all the more reason for hastening the recruitment and training of our militia units," William Hendricks added.

"Well, we've had a very encouraging start," Captain Innes said with a smile. "Once Patrick Henry announced he wished to command a regiment, men have been flocking to join! In just a month, all the regular companies and all the militia companies had filled their ranks!" Then his face grew serious. "But recruiting men is one thing; training them to fight the regular British army is another! Now we've got to train those men to fight in a disciplined way. Many are skilled marksmen —but they've got to learn to fight in companies."

George Wythe looked keenly at Captain Innes. "James, you expressed to me some reservations about Mr. Henry's appointment as Colonel of Virginia's First Regiment."

Capt. Innes flushed. He took a moment to reply, and Andrew realized that he was choosing his words with great care. Andrew wondered why anyone would hesitate to put the great Patrick Henry in command of the militia formations. He was about to learn.

Captain Innes cleared his throat. Then he spoke softly. "Gentlemen, no one in Virginia admires Mr. Henry more than I." He paused, and used the time to light up a long clay pipe. Then he continued. "And it does Henry credit to volunteer to fight. Only—he's a statesman, not a soldier. Perhaps the greatest statesman in all the colonies. His experience is in the legislature—not the field. He's not fought Indians, nor French, before. No one doubts his courage. But some of us think he's best suited as a leader in our government, not in our army. Look how well he's led us since 1765! And we can't help wishing he'd stay where he's proved himself to be so effective!"

"You're quite right!" George Wythe replied quietly. "Some of us think Patrick Henry is one of the greatest men of this age.

But, like you, James, many of us also wish he'd stayed in the legislature, where we need him. We wish he'd left military leadership to men more experienced in war than he."

As if by common consent, the men changed the topic. When Patrick Henry had announced that he'd like to be Colonel of Virginia's First Regiment, objections had been raised at once. Some of his best friends—including George Washington— were embarrassed by Henry's effort to secure military command. They hesitated to oppose him in any way, but they wished that he had chosen to remain in political office, where he had proved himself to be one of Virginia's greatest and most effective statesman.

But many others had replied that Henry would not have offered himself for the post if he hadn't been confident that with good advisors he would learn the job and acquit himself with honor. His presence had indeed been a powerful drawing card for enlistments—over a thousand recruits were already camped around the town of Williamsburg.

George Wythe changed the subject by asking Captain Innes about the state of training of the various militia units. Half an hour later, the men separated. Andrew and his father rode home, dismounted in back of the house, and entered the office.

CHAPTER THREE

Take These Supplies to the Militia

When Andrew followed his father into the office building, he found his sister, Rachel, and her friend, Sarah Edwards, talking with Sarah's father.

"Here's the hero of the hour!" Nelson Edwards beamed, rising from his chair and grasping Andrew's hand in his powerful grip. "Your sister has been trying to tell me about your ride last night, but she can't seem to remember much about it!"

"But, Mr. Edwards," Rachel Hendricks protested, "this is the first time I've seen him today! He came in before dawn, mother said, and went to bed. Then he slept all day! I haven't even seen him! I was just trying to remember the little bit mother told me!"

Edwards laughed, bright blue eyes beaming under eyebrows that were as dark as the thick hair on his head. "Well, I guess he'd earned that sleep." Edwards was a thick-set man, powerful, with no fat at all on his stocky frame.

"He had, indeed!!" William Hendricks added with a smile. "But that's no excuse for his not working now—what have we got for him to do, Nelson?"

"Actually, William," Nelson Edwards replied, "I'd like him to take a wagon-load of supplies to the militia camp behind the College grounds. The wagon's loaded and waiting. I told Colonel Henry's officer that we'd deliver it within two hours."

"Can Sarah and I go with him, Father?" Rachel asked quickly. "After all, we haven't had a chance to talk with him at all! Please, Father!"

Andrew's sister Rachel was slender, with light brown hair and brown eyes. Today she was dressed in a green dress, and, like Sarah and the other women and girls of the colony, she wore a white cap on her head.

"Go with Andrew?" William Hendricks asked, puzzled, glancing quickly at Nelson Edwards. "What do you think, Nelson? Ordinarily I'd not want the girls to get close to the militia camps."

"Neither would I," Nelson Edwards replied. "But the wagon's going to deliver its load to a building on the Richmond Road two blocks this side of the camp. I think it might be all right—especially since they'll be with Andrew." He threw a shrewd glance at his daughter, Sarah, who blushed and glanced away.

William Hendricks saw his friend's quick glance, saw the eager question in Andrew's eyes, and made a quick decision. "Let the girls go with him, then. They'll help keep him out of trouble!"

A few minutes later, four horses pulled the big wagon away from the warehouse behind Hendrick's and Edwards' office, and headed toward the College of William and Mary. It was cold this October day, and both girls wore their cloaks over their woolen dresses. Andrew wore a deerskin jacket that reached below his belt. Sarah rode between Andrew and Rachel, and the two girls plied Andrew with question after question as he guided the wagon through the busy streets of Williamsburg.

"Did you really have to fight a British officer?" Sarah asked, blue eyes wide.

Andrew hesitated. He'd not told his mother much about the fight with the officer; hadn't wanted to say anything that would make her worry, in fact. But he knew that his father would tell her eventually, so he'd described the chase, the fall his horse had taken, and the tomahawk throw that had brought down his pursuer and enabled him finally to escape with the message he carried.

"Well," he said finally, "a British officer tried to stop me last night, but I got away."

"But did you *fight* him, I asked?" Sarah repeated, becoming exasperated at Andrew's evasiveness. "Honestly, Andrew, sometimes I get the feeling that you don't want to tell me and Rachel *anything*!" Andrew was strangely disconcerted to have her sitting so close beside him on the wagon seat; Rachel had somehow maneuvered Sarah between them—on purpose, Andrew knew.

Rachel's just trying to aggravate me! he thought to himself.

"Andrew, tell the truth!" Rachel said hotly, bringing Andrew out of his thoughts with a jerk. "I **know** you had to fight that man! Now, tell us what happened!"

Andrew sighed resignedly. "Well," he said slowly, "I got the message from our scout after sunset. It was urgent—the

British were sending three boatloads of men to attack another river plantation, and steal the cannon our militia had stored there. Our spies learned where they planned to attack, and my job was to take that message to some men who were waiting in a boat by the river. But I had to go slow because it was so dark, and I couldn't see the road very well—and neither could *Dusty*! But I thought I was going to get away without any trouble with the British or the Tories."

"What happened?" Rachel asked.

"Just when I thought I'd gotten past the British patrols, a bunch of soldiers rode out of the trees right in front of me and ordered me to stop!"

"What did you do?" Sarah asked breathlessly.

"I kicked the horse into a run! I didn't even think about it—I just kicked him into a run, and *Dusty* broke through the whole group! He knocked down a big horse, and threw the rider to the ground, too! That's the last thing they were expecting me to do! Then I galloped down that dark road, praying *Dusty* wouldn't break his leg in a pothole! When I came to a fork, I took it, thinking it would throw them off my trail."

"Did it?" Rachel asked.

"Nope. At least, it didn't fool the officer. But maybe it fooled his men, "cause they never showed up. Anyway, I rode down a real narrow path and then came out into a clearing. I pulled up, "cause at first I couldn't see the path on the other side. And that's when *Dusty* stumbled and went down!"

"Did you jump clear?" Sarah asked, her eyes wide, and disconcertingly close to his own. She knew that a falling horse often pinned its rider beneath it.

"Yes," he answered, looking away quickly, "I jumped clear. And I jumped back on my feet. But just then a horse galloped out from the path I'd just left. When I turned around, that Britisher had burst out of the trees and fired his pistol at me. Then he was riding straight at me, yelling something fierce, his sabre ready to cut me in half!" Andrew shuddered at the memory of that long blade flashing in the moonlight.

"What did you do then?" Rachel asked. She hadn't realized how deadly the situation had been for her brother, and now she was sorry she'd been so impatient with him.

"My rifle was in its scabbard on the horse, and my pistol was in the holster by the saddle. And *Dusty* was on the other side of the clearing, out of my reach. All I had on me was my tomahawk and long knife. So I threw my tomahawk and knocked the Britisher off his horse."

"Thank the Lord for that, Andrew!" Sarah said. She was horrified at the danger he'd been in, and her face, so close to his own, could not conceal her fear.

Andrew looked quickly ahead. "Well," he said, "I ran over and pulled my tomahawk out of the man's chest. He was alive, but he was breathing badly, and he didn't get up. My next problem was to catch *Dusty*. He'd jumped up after his fall—he wasn't really hurt, but he did have a limp—and I had to coax him to let me get in the saddle again. Any minute I thought the other British soldiers would ride into the clearing and catch me!"

"Where were they?" Rachel asked, leaning forward so she could look past Sarah at her brother.

"I don't know," Andrew said. "I think they must not have seen their officer take that turn to follow me. They must have been farther behind, and I bet they kept going on the road. That's the only thing I can think of. And it's the only reason I got away!"

Now the wagon had reached the broad Duke of Gloucester Street. Andrew pulled the horses into a wide left turn, and the wagon headed toward the College of William and Mary at the far end of the street. With the coming of over a thousand militiamen to guard the city from British attack, many horsemen, and many supply wagons, were in the road, and their passage was slow. Andrew didn't mind. He wanted the trip to last until dark!

"There's the Printing Office," Rachel observed, as they rode past the small brick building that housed not only a printing business, but also a book store and a Post Office. Sarah and Rachel had spent many hours poring over books in that store.

"Every time we come by there, I remember the day we heard those ladies talking about the Governor's plans," Sarah said, frowning. "That's where we overheard Mrs. Granville tell of the dreadful plan to capture Mr. Patrick Henry!"

"And we almost didn't get away from the Governor's men she sent to catch us!" Rachel added. "If you and Nathan hadn't rescued us, Andrew, there's no telling what might have happened!"

"That was your idea, wasn't it, Andrew?" Sarah asked, her eyes shining. "For you and Nathan to pretend to fight each other—so you could get in the way of those men who were chasing us?"

"Well, we had to do *something*," he answered. "I thought if we got right in their path, and faked a fight, we could hold them up long enough for you two to escape."

"It worked, all right!" Rachel said gratefully. "But, imagine—the Governor was planning to capture Mr. Patrick Henry and send him to England for trial!"

"For hanging, you mean!" Andrew said. "That's the same thing the British planned to do with Mr. John Hancock and Mr. Samuel Adams up in Massachusetts! And that's when Mr. Paul Revere rode out from Boston and warned the Patriots. He and other riders took the message that the British troops were coming to capture the Patriot leaders and destroy the Patriot cannon and military stores!"

"That's when the militiamen fought them at Lexington and Concord, wasn't it?" Sarah asked.

"That's right!" Andrew said. "And they drove the British troops back to Boston in terrible shape. They almost captured them all. But a regiment of British marines came just in time to rescue the redcoats. That marine commander was real smart, and fought a brilliant retreat. He brought his men back to Cambridge before the Massachusetts militia could surround them, and got them back just in time."

"Look, there's a crowd of people at Bruton Parish Church," Rachel observed, pointing ahead and to their right.

"Looks like a bunch of new militia recruits," Andrew said. "They're handing out muskets and powder horns and cartridge boxes."

The magnificent red brick church loomed closer. Built in 1715, the building was, and had long been a landmark in the town.

"That church tower's only five years old, I think," Sarah said.

"It's pretty," Rachel commented. "Some people think it should have been made of brick like the rest of the church, but I like the wood."

A pack of dogs burst around the far wall of the church yard and poured into the street just ahead of them! The four startled horses snorted wildly, veered to the left, and almost tore the reins out of Andrew's hands as they pulled the wagon into the middle of the street, straight toward a long freight wagon coming from the other direction. The girls grabbed the wagon seat to keep from falling out, as Andrew gripped the reins with all his strength and hauled the horses back to the right. It was a real struggle, but finally the horses settled down.

The dogs, meanwhile, barking madly, boiled across the street, wreaked havoc along the hitching rail, and caused several horses to break free and bolt away.

Men were shouting at the dogs, but to no avail. Barking wildly, the pack raced along the other side of the road, leaving chaos in their path!

"Why don't they keep those dogs tied?" Sarah exclaimed, her face flushed from the sudden fright.

"They can't," Andrew replied. "There's too many of 'em. Every new batch of militia seems to bring more dogs to town. Mr. Patrick Henry's ordered his men to camp out behind the College, to keep 'em out of the middle of town, but there's still a lot of traffic on the streets."

Now they were approaching the College of William and Mary. The stately college building, believed to have been designed by Sir Christopher Wren, was flanked on either side by two beautiful three storey houses. The one on their right was the home of the President of the College, and the other, on the left, was called The Brafferton.

"Where do your friends Moses and Abraham live?" Rachel asked.

"In the Brafferton," Andrew answered. That's the house to our left. There's maybe a dozen Indian boys there now, studying."

"Who pays their expenses?" Sarah asked.

"That's an interesting story," Andrew replied. "Moses and Abraham told Nathan and me all about it. A famous English scientist, Sir Robert Boyle, died maybe eighty years ago, and left a lot of money for education and charities. Mr. James Blair persuaded Mr. Boyle's executors to give a lot of the money to pay for Indian boys to be educated in the College, so they could go back to their tribes and convert their people to the Lord. There have always been Indian boys here, studying with the other students."

"Mr. Blair started the College, didn't he?" Sarah asked.

"He sure did," Andrew answered. "The Virginia General Assembly sent him to England to persuade King William and Queen Mary to give money to start the College. Then he persuaded other people to give money for it. He was the first President of the College, and a great man, Father says. And he left a lot of money to his brother's son John Blair, Jr.—who's a real Patriot! He's a member of the House of Burgesses right now."

Now the wagon had come to the fork where the roads divided, just before the grounds of the College. This was a busy part of town; stores and shops flanked Duke of Gloucester street on either side, wagons and horses were tethered in front of the stores. Traffic slowed as the broad street met the two forks. The road to the left went past the College to Jamestown; the road to the right went by the other side of the College, and on to Richmond. Andrew pulled the horses to the right, and the wagon lumbered over the rough road and began to pass the College buildings.

There was more traffic here: wagons, horsemen, and men on foot. And a lot of men in militia uniform; these wore hunting shirts over long leggings, wide belts that crossed their shoulders holding knives and powder horns and cartridge boxes and tomahawks. Dust rose from the many hooves of the horses and wheels of the wagons, and Andrew concentrated on keeping his nervous horses under tight rein.

"We're almost there," he said. "We'll turn behind that white house on the right, and stop in the yard behind." He was pleased to see that the traffic was not so thick once he'd passed the fork in the road.

"There's Jed!" Rachel said suddenly, alarmed at the sight of the big bully.

"He's got two friends with him!" Sarah said fearfully.

"He won't cause any trouble," Andrew said confidently, "not with all these men around."

Andrew was wrong.

CHAPTER FOUR

The Fight

Jed Marks was a bully. He was big, bigger than most everyone his age, and he'd learned early in life that he could beat up on the smaller boys. Now, at seventeen, he was a grown man; but he was just as mean and irresponsible as he'd always been.

Jed had no father. In fact, Jed didn't even know who his father was. Tragically, after Jed had been born, his mother had taken up with a succession of worthless men. Jed had never known the love and firm guidance of a good man. As he grew up, his mother took in laundry and sewing to support herself and her son. But her own loose ways, and her worthless men, had given the boy a terrible example. Without good male guidance and supervision, Jed had become a bully.

"Look at him!" Sarah exclaimed, eyes wide with shock. "He's dressed like a Patriot! The hypocrite!"

She and Rachel were stunned. Just a few months before, Jed had accosted them as they returned home from their violin lesson. He'd taunted them then with the news that a British fleet would bring a British army to force Virginia into subjection to the Crown. And then he'd demanded that the two girls treat him with respect.

The girls knew then that he despised the Patriot cause. Now, their astonished gaze took in his hunting shirt, with the words, "Liberty Or Death", blazoned across a wide band on his chest.

This was the battle cry many Virginia militiamen wore on their hunting shirts, and was a phrase taken from the famous speech Patrick Henry had delivered a few months before.

"How can that bully wear a Patriot shirt?" Sarah asked disgustedly.

"He's just currying favor with the town right now," Andrew said grimly. "He knows that most folk in Williamsburg want liberty for the colonies!"

"Well, he's a liar!" Rachel said angrily. "We know he's a British sympathizer! He told us so himself!"

Jed had seen them! Speaking quickly to the men beside him, he advanced toward the wagon, a wicked grin on his wide face. His small grey eyes glinted with perverse pleasure as he saw Andrew and the girls approach. His friends came with him, one on either side. The two were as big as Jed, Andrew noted.

Andrew could not move the wagon away from the approaching men. Two wagons coming from the direction of Richmond blocked the road on the other side; he had to stay in the right hand lane of the road.

Andrew's face grew grim as the trio drew nearer. "Don't say anything, girls," he said. "No matter what he says, don't answer. Let me talk."

Andrew still didn't think Jed and his friends would do anything to trouble a wagon with girls aboard—not in the presence of other wagons and men in the street. But he underestimated Jed and his vindictiveness.

For Jed didn't intend to say anything at all—not at first, that is. He simply came up to the lead right-hand horse of Andrew's wagon, screamed into the animal's ears, and waved his hat in front of the beast's startled eyes.

The frightened horse reared back on his hind legs, throwing the animal beside him off balance. Then he broke into a sudden gallop—before the other horses were ready to move. Dreadful confusion broke out as the wildly neighing animals struggled to keep their balance while the lead horse was pulling them ahead.

The girls fell against each other on the wagon seat as the four horses finally broke into a run. Desperately Andrew guided them into the middle of the road, hauling back on the reins with all his strength, trying to bring them to a halt.

At once, Jed and his friends ran beside the wagon, appearing to try to help, but actually yelling at the horses to keep them alarmed. Now the wagon was bouncing in the middle of the road, between some wagons and horses coming from Richmond and the line of traffic leaving Williamsburg. Sarah and Rachel struggled to keep from falling backwards into the cargo behind them, and slammed against a row of barrels that swayed with the violent motion of the lurching wagon.

Within fifty yards, Andrew pulled the horses out of their mad gallop into a trot. Then he slowed them to a walk. Seeing a gap in the line of wagons, he pulled his wagon over to the side of the road, and out of the lane of traffic. Yanking back the long wooden handle that braked the wagon, the infuriated boy leaped to the ground.

"Get down!" he called urgently. Reaching up, he grabbed his sister's hand, and helped the shaking girl out of the wagon. Sarah came next. Just as she reached the ground, Rachel screamed.

"Andrew!" she cried.

Whirling, Andrew was just in time to dodge one of the big men who'd run up with Jed. The man lurched by, fist swinging. Andrew ducked under the blow and swept his left foot in a vicious arc that knocked the man's leg out from under him. As the man began to fall, Andrew planted his feet, whipped his body around from the hip, and smashed his right fist against the attacker's jaw with all his force. A bone cracked as the man crashed to the ground.

Then Andrew whirled back to face Jed, who was running right at him. Andrew sidestepped at the last moment, slapped aside Jed's left fist with his right hand, and clubbed his own left hand twice into the big man's ribs as he hurtled by. Jed crashed to the ground, gasping with pain and hugging his side.

The third man ground to a stop in front of Andrew, wary now that his two friends had been knocked down, nervously watching the boy to see what he would do. Andrew stepped toward him, and the man turned and ran—right into a crowd of men who'd rushed up from a militia unit across the road.

Andrew whirled to face the two men he'd knocked down, half expecting to be hit from behind as he turned. But Jed was still on the ground, writhing in pain, crying out that his rib was broken. The first attacker, hand gripped to his jaw, struggled to his feet in time to see Andrew knock down Jed, then see his other friend run away. He decided that he too had had enough, and whirled around to escape. But he ran straight into a crowd of militia; the men grabbed him and held him fast.

Now a crowd of militiamen swarmed around them, drawn by the cries of the two girls. They arrived in time to see Sarah grab an axe handle from a barrel on the wagon and rush toward Jed. Hastily, two men stopped her.

"Whoa, Young Lady," one of them said, "don't kill him! Your young friend has already hurt him pretty bad!"

They pried the axe handle gently from the hands of the struggling girl, then turned her toward Andrew. "See here, now, the boy's all right! He don't need no help whipping those men! Your young man can fight, Miss!"

Two men yanked Jed roughly to his feet, as others held fast the man whose jaw Andrew had broken. Jed was groaning, bent over and holding his left side. His friend was clutching his dirty sleeve to his face to stop the flow of blood from his mouth.

"Let's take these three to the gaol!" one of the men said grimly. "We saw 'em spook the horses—and with girls aboard the wagon!"

The militiamen were outraged—women and girls weren't treated that way in Virginia. Jed and his friends would most likely reach the goal with more blows and bruises from the angered men; already the militiamen were punishing them as they hauled them along, ignoring their victims' cries.

Jed fell down suddenly. The men grabbed him again, hauled him roughly to his feet once more, hit him several times with great force, then lifted him and threw him violently into a wagon.

"Don't you young folks worry about him," a big man said to Andrew and the girls. "We're taking all three of 'em to the gaol. We'll find the sheriff and tell him just what we saw. You come down later, Boy, and tell what happened. Next time you see any of 'em, they'll be in the stocks!"

"That was fine fightin', Young Man," another said to Andrew, as a crowd of men took Jed and his companions away.

"Oh, Andrew!" Sarah said. "Are you all right?" She and Rachel rushed to him.

"I reckon so," he replied, chest heaving as he drew in deep breaths. He was enraged still at the danger Jed and his men had brought to the girls—spooking the horses into a run as they had! He and the girls could have been badly injured. Andrew regretted that he hadn't been able to hit Jed's other friend.

Neither Andrew nor Sarah nor Rachel saw the two young men standing in the yard next to the house before which the wagon had halted. Stephen Bancroft was tall, broad-shouldered, and powerfully built, with blond hair atop his nobly formed head. His father was a merchant in Williamsburg, working for a Scotch firm with warehouses in Norfolk. Father and son had lately come under suspicion from the Patriots when Stephen had been discovered carrying messages from his father to the Governor's spies.

The Bancroft's situation was made worse when other letters from Norfolk merchants to their superiors in England were intercepted by the Patriots. These letters revealed that the British merchant companies had given the King's Government a huge sum of money to finance Britain's military campaign to suppress Virginia's movement toward independence! The Patriots were outraged at this information, and outraged at the merchants and British sympathizers in Norfolk who used the money they got from their businesses in Virginia to finance the enslavement of the Colony.

Mr. Bancroft and his son Stephen had been warned with great severity that they had better not do anything further to harm the Patriot cause. The Bancrofts gave their promise, and were allowed to go free.

Stephen had never forgiven Sarah and Rachel for reporting him to Captain Innes of the Williamsburg militia. They were the ones who had overheard his conversation with the Governor's spy, thus bringing him and his father to the hostile attention of the Patriots. Stephen had determined to revenge himself on the girls somehow.

Now, as Stephen saw Andrew knock down Jed and his crony, his rage knew no bounds.

"John!" he said to his companion. "That's Andrew Hendricks! And those girls with him are Sarah Edwards and Rachel Hendricks, the girls that turned me in to Captain Innes and the militia company!" he snarled bitterly. "One of our spies in the militia told me how I'd gotten caught—it was because of those two girls! They overheard you and me talking outside Mrs. Gardiner's house, when you brought me that message, and their fathers set the militia on me. Papa's already lost a lot of customers since they found out he's on the side of the King! He'll be ruined, he says! All because of those girls!"

John frowned in anger. "When will the Governor let us bring those girls to the ship? They're Patriot spies, and he knows it! They're the same girls who overheard that the Governor planned to capture Patrick Henry! They passed the message to Henry, and he got away! Surely the Governor won't let them keep spying against him!"

"He's afraid to kidnap girls from Williamsburg," Stephen said bitterly. "Said that gentlemen didn't do such things. Said the whole Colony would rise against him if people heard that he'd done such a deed! Said two young girls couldn't cause that much trouble anyway, and accused me and father of exaggerating their importance! He forgot that they almost got the two of us gaoled!"

"Well, *something's* got to be done about 'em!" John snarled. "But not when they're with that boy! Someone taught him how to *fight!* You saw him whip Jed and his friends just now!"

"Yeah, but that's "cause they were fools and came at him one at a time. If they can't fight any better than that, they should have jumped him all together!"

John looked keenly at Stephen. "You could whip him, couldn't you?"

Stephen was tall, broad-shouldered, quick on his feet, and exceptionally skilled at boxing. John had seen him beat larger men to a pulp during game days in the city.

"I sure could!" Stephen snapped grimly. "I will, too! Soon's I get the chance!"

"Get back!" John warned suddenly. "Some of those militiamen are lookin' this way!"

The two men stepped back behind the building, then turned and hurried off. John and Stephen had come to spy on the militia companies camped behind the College. But the scene with Jed and the girls on the wagon, and then the fight, had brought too many militiamen running toward them. They realized that they couldn't afford to be caught so near the militia camps, so they stepped quickly away, and headed back toward the middle of town.

"I think I've got an idea!" Stephen said, as they crossed the street. "I think I know how we can get one of those girls and question her. *Then* we'll learn just what they're really doing for the Patriots, and how they seem to get word to their leaders."

"Won't that be dangerous?"

Stephen smiled. "Nah! Those Patriots think they're smart, using girls as spies, thinking no one would suspect 'em. We'll show 'em whose smart!"

Half-an-hour later, Andrew pulled the empty wagon out into the nearly deserted road and into a wide turn, then headed toward home. Sarah and Rachel were beside him as before. Dark was falling, and with the setting of the sun the temperature had fallen sharply as well. The girls wrapped themselves in their capes against the cold, and pulled their capes over their heads. The three huddled close together for warmth. Andrew had put on his long jacket and tricorn hat.

"Those men took their time unloading the wagon!" Sarah observed.

"They were too busy looking at you girls," Andrew grinned. "That's all these militiamen seem to do—flirt with the women in town! Lots of them are from out in the country, you know, and they've never seen so many girls. 'Specially not pretty ones like you two!"

"Andrew!" Rachel said.

"That's nonsense!" Sarah added.

But they all knew that the militiamen were having somewhat of a picnic in Williamsburg. There was no fighting to do, only training, and the officers couldn't keep their men busy all the time. So the men pulled lots of pranks, shot off their muskets to frighten women who passed by, and generally had themselves a fine time. That was one reason Patrick Henry had pulled his men out of the town itself and camped them in the fields behind the College of William and Mary.

"I hope that big redheaded man back there didn't break his toes when the barrel fell on 'em!" Sarah said.

"Well, if you two hadn't been flirtin' with him, he would have watched what he was doing and wouldn't have dropped it!" Andrew said, trying to look serious. "Honest, girls, you can't cut your eyes at men like that, or you'll distract 'em and then someone'll get hurt!"

"Andrew!" both girls protested at once, really provoked. It was untrue, and Andrew knew it, but he couldn't resist teasing them.

Rachel suddenly changed the subject. "You don't think Jed and those bullies are waiting for us, do you?" she asked with an anxious frown, scanning the road ahead in the gathering dark.

"No, I don't," Andrew said firmly. "Those militiamen meant business. The won't let Jed get away with that dangerous stunt—scarin' the horses with you girls in the wagon! They probably beat him and his friends on the way to gaol. They sure were going to have 'em locked up—we won't see 'em at all! Father will take this to the sheriff, too, and Jed knows it.

Thus reassured, the three began to enjoy the ending of the day and the pleasant—though cold—ride home. The girls were rarely away from their homes at the approach of dark, especially not since the arrival of the militia companies. Now they enjoyed the feeling of adventure. Lights began to shine in the windows of the houses as they rode back along Duke of Gloucester Street, and there were fewer people in sight. The girls loved to look in the windows of the homes as they passed. The clop-clop-clop of the horses hooves and the rumbling of the big wagon wheels marked their peaceful passage through the town.

They passed the Powder Magazine, then went past the Market Square Tavern, and kept on until they reached the next corner. Here Andrew turned the wagon to the right, off the broad street, onto the road leading toward their home. Sometimes the wheels broke a stone with a sharp *crack*. A couple of dogs barked briefly at them, then grew quiet. The darkness deepened, the cold increased, and the three huddled closer together for warmth. Andrew was sorry when Sarah's house, and then his own, came in view.

Andrew turned the wagon past their homes, and into the yard behind, where their fathers' office and barn and warehouse stood dimly in the falling dark. He pulled to a stop, jumped to the ground, then reached up and helped the girls down from the high wagon seat. They thanked him, and hurried into their homes, bursting to tell of their adventures and Andrew's fight with Jed and his men.

Andrew unharnessed the animals and led them into the barn. One of his father's hired men was still working, and the two of them rubbed the animals down and fed them. Then Andrew trudged to his house, stepped up to the back porch, and opened the kitchen door.

A cheerful light shone through the window, and he could smell something cooking.

I'm starved! he thought. And he was tired too, he realized suddenly. He'd had a long day: he'd had the fight with Jed, he'd worked with the militiamen to unload the heavy barrels from the wagon, he'd been constantly vigilant watching for trouble on the way home (without telling the girls!). Now he was ready to call it a day.

☆ CHAPTER FIVE ☆

Dunmore Strikes Again!

The marauding British warships had captured several merchant vessels owned by the colonists. One of these was the *Eilbeck,* which Governor Dunmore (with typical humility) promptly renamed after himself: *H.M.S Dunmore*! This day he'd called the captains of the other ships, as well as the available British Army officers, to meet in the great cabin of his new flagship.

Dunmore—Earl John Murray was his proper title—was a powerfully built Scotsman, an athlete, and an avid hunter. He was utterly loyal to his King. Dunmore had fled with his family from the Palace in Williamsburg, convinced that the Patriots meant to capture him and his family and hold them hostage. This is what Dunmore himself had publically threatened to do with Patrick Henry and other Virginia leaders, and he fully expected the Virginians to do the same to him if they had the chance. He determined not to give them the chance, and took refuge with the small British warships stationed off Norfolk.

Shortly after finding safety on board a British warship, the Governor had switched his headquarters to the more spacious quarters of this captured merchantman. He'd then planned a number of successful raids on Virginia farms and plantations, leading some of these raids himself. The aim of these attacks was to capture Patriot cannon and destroy Patriot munitions.

The cannon he was seeking to capture had been taken by Virginians in past wars with France and were now stored by the Patriots for the defense of Virginia. Dunmore meant to capture or destroy them so that they could not be used by Virginia against the forces of the King. He also wanted to demonstrate to Virginians the great power of the British Empire, and thus intimidate them into remaining loyal to King George.

The small British Navy squadron under Lord Dunmore's command was anchored off the town of Norfolk, many of whose citizens were open supporters of the King. Many of Norfolk's inhabitants had been thoroughly intimidated by Dunmore's forces, and their militia unit of two hundred men had fled without a fight when the British troops marched toward them. All of the coastal towns, in fact, were inclined to resist the move toward independence from Great Britain: their nearness to the sea made them too vulnerable to the guns of the British warships and landing parties! And they'd heard that the British Navy had already burned down towns in other coastal colonies to the north.

Yet a sizeable number of citizens even in the coastal towns thought differently than Dunmore; they favored independence from the tyranny of the King and Parliament. And their numbers were such that many people loyal to the King were persuaded to leave their homes and take refuge on merchant ships moored off-shore—just in case Virginia's resistance proved successful.

Now, in the cabin of the merchantman-turned-warship, Dunmore planned further raids against the Patriots' caches of artillery. With him this morning were Captain Samuel Leslie of the 14th Regiment and the captains of his small warships: the newly christened *Dunmore, King's Fisher, Otter,* and *William.*

The low-ceilinged cabin was damp and cold this October day, and stuffy with the smoke of the mens' long clay pipes. The officers huddled around a thick wooden table on which Dunmore had spread a map of the adjacent coastline of Virginia. Here, against the background noise of the creaking of the ship's timbers and the thudding of sailors' feet on the wooden deck above, the former Governor of Virginia had plotted the next British attacks.

"Our troops captured nineteen cannon from Joseph Hutchings' place!" Dunmore gloated, "and fifty more from the other farms. That's most all of the artillery those rebels had saved from the wars with the French and with the pirates! Soon they'll have only their muskets and rifles with which to fight us!"

Governor Dunmore was a powerfully built man in the prime of life. He bore himself with the easy assurance of wealth and power, and the smooth grace of an athlete. Dunmore was a fighting man, a decisive leader—but a man given easily to anger. His subordinates feared to cross him.

Captain Leslie, however, was not as pleased as was Dunmore with their efforts to quell the rebellion, and thought he should register his concerns.

"I wish we'd gotten that load of gunpowder the Goodriches brought into Kemp's landing!" Leslie complained bitterly. "The rebels have a critical shortage of gunpowder, and those barrels of powder will help them a great deal."

Leslie had helped the Governor plan that raid, and he was particularly disturbed at its failure. His own report to London was not nearly as optimistic as the report Dunmore had sent. Leslie had written to his superiors that there was a very large number of Virginians armed, ready, and willing to fight for their independence, and that it would take a powerful British force to bring the Colony back into submission to the Crown.

"Don't worry, Captain!" Dummore said, his thick face determined and very confident. "We may have just a few ships, but we've got enough to stop those rebels from getting any weapons and powder through these ports. But now, I want to destroy the town of Hampton, to teach those rebels a lesson! I want our ships to shell and burn down every house our naval cannon can reach!"

"Didn't the Virginians sink some ships in the channel to block our approach to that town?" the captain of the *Otter* asked in surprise. "We can't risk sinking our own vessels on those obstacles!"

"You can get around them!" the Governor snapped impatiently. Dunmore did not appreciate objections to his plans. "You'll sneak up on 'em at night, slip through those sunken hulks, and bombard the town in the morning! Don't leave a rebel house standing!"

The naval captains looked at each other nervously, although no one said anything. But an hour later, as they left the cabin and went up on deck to take their small boats back to their own ships, the British officers huddled against the rail to discuss the Governor's orders.

"The Governor's a soldier!" the captain of *H.M.S. William* said. "He doesn't know what it means to strike our ships' hulls against a sunken vessel!"

"I'm not going to try getting through that barrier without sending out small boats to find a clear passage!" Captain Squire of *H.M.S. Otter* said decisively.

The captains all agreed to this elementary naval precaution which had eluded the soldierly mind of the Governor. Frowning with concern, the officers climbed down the ship's side into their waiting boats, and were rowed back to their own commands.

Later, when dark had fallen, the British squadron of five vessels approached the small town of Hampton. But, as their captains had feared, they found that the ships the Virginians had sunk in the channel prevented their own vessels from getting close to the town. Frustrated, they landed a party of men in small boats to raid some houses and bring back prisoners.

The next morning, the soldiers that the ships had landed fought a sharp fight with two companies of Virginia militia. The redcoats then succeeded in burning a farmhouse on Cooper's Plantation on the Hampton River. Smoke towered into the sky as the victorious redcoats and Loyalists marched away; the flames and smoke served as a grim warning to other Virginians in Hampton and the surrounding countryside.

The next night, as the river was cloaked with darkness, the sounds of small boats could be heard across the water. Slowly the boats were rowed toward the line of sunken hulls in the river. Sailors with axes began to chop those timbers that stuck out of the water. Doggedly the boats hacked their way through the masts and spars of the sunken ships, clearing a path so that their own vessels could approach the town in the morning.

When dawn broke, the waiting Virginian militiamen on shore saw that the five British ships were within cannon range of their town. They heard across the water the unmistakable sounds of warships preparing for battle. The British plan was to fire red-hot cannonballs at the houses and buildings in Hampton, and thus burn the small town to the ground. The ships' drummers beat the staccato call to battle stations, the crews raced to their stations, the cannons were loaded and run out of the opened gun-ports, and the gunners prepared to start the bombardment that would destroy the town.

"Take your last look at those houses and buildings, Gentlemen!" Dunmore said to the officers nearby. "You won't see 'em in an hour! There won't be anything left but piles of burning rubble!"

Suddenly, the British officers and crew saw puffs of smoke erupt from the houses and from behind fences on shore. Sailors on the decks of the British ships cried out and fell as the sound of the deadly Virginian rifles burst across the water. Other rifles fired, and soon, as men reloaded, there was a continuous firing directed at the British crews.

During the night, and unknown to the British, Colonel Woodford of the Second Virginia Regiment had led a group of riflemen into Hampton. The men had taken position in houses and behind fences while it was still dark. When the warships approached in the morning, these riflemen fired with such deadly accuracy that the British sailors could not remain on deck to man their ships' cannons! The sailors had to flee the guns and take cover below—or be shot down! The marksmen on shore kept peppering the decks of the British ships, until the vessels were forced to sail away. The attack on Hampton had been repulsed.

The *Hawk*, a small boat from the sloop *Otter,* had ten men and its skipper brought down by the murderous rifle fire. The vessel lost control, and ran aground.

Aboard the newly-christened *H.M.S. Dunmore,* the Governor burst into his cabin in a towering rage at the humiliating defeat of his ships by Virginia riflemen. He threw himself into a chair, face red with fury, eyes bulging, thick veins in his neck throbbing. Then his temper erupted like a volcano and he lost all control. Pounding the table with his thick fists he shouted that he'd get revenge.

Later, when the small flotilla had come to anchor back in Norfolk, he called another council of war in the ship's cabin.

Again the ships' captains were rowed from their vessels to *H.M.S. Dunmore.* Again they climbed up the ship's side and stepped onto its deck. And again they entered the large cabin at the vessel's stern. Here Dunmore was waiting for them, his thick red face agleam with his new plan to trouble the rebellious Virginians.

"We'll move to the south," he said, pointing to the map spread once more on the thick wooden table. "A band of rebel militia from North Carolina is marching toward Great Bridge, south of Kemp's Landing. The Virginians have militia facing our fort at Great Bridge, and when the Carolinians join them, they mean to attack us."

He swept his hand across the map, and pointed toward Virginia's former capitol. "We'll keep the *King's Fisher* just off Jamestown, to prevent the Virginians from crossing reinforcements to the southern side of the river. Then we'll land our men at Kemp's Landing and attack the Virginia militia before those North Carolina militia can reinforce them! Then we'll march quickly and destroy the North Carolinians!"

With sudden violence he slammed his thick fist on the table. "We'll strike these rebel formations one at a time, before they can gather and help each other! That's what our sea power does for us—lets us land where we will, without warning, and attack where we choose! We'll crush this rebellion in short order!"

Dunmore's plan was sound, and his officers knew it. The Virginians as yet had no warships—but the British did. That gave the King's forces command of the vital rivers, and gave them also the capacity to launch quick raids anywhere they wished, before the Virginians could mobilize to oppose them. If Great Britain were to send more ships and regiments of soldiers—as Dunmore had begged London to do—his forces might so damage Virginia's power to fight that the rebellious American colonies could well be cut in two! Virginia was the largest of the colonies, and was a great producer of food, as well as a great source of armed men.

"If we can recapture Virginia," Dunmore argued, "the entire rebellion might be quelled within a year. Especially if our agents succeed in buying the allegiance of the Indian tribes to the west! Those tribes will set the border aflame with fire and torture, draw the best Virginia riflemen to defend the settlers, and thus divide Virginia's forces! We'll attack from the Atlantic, the Indians will swoop in from the West, and together we'll crush the rebellion!"

The naval captains nodded agreement with Dunmore's plan. Stubborn and difficult as he was to work with, he was an aggressive and far-sighted strategist, and this time his plan, they knew, was sound. If they could win some initial victories, the government in London might be persuaded to throw naval and military forces to Dunmore's support: they well might crush the rebellion this year!

At least the rebellion in Virginia.

In Williamsburg, the Patriot leaders faced difficult deci-
sions. There was still great concern about the role of Patrick
Henry in the Virginia military. Officially, he'd been voted in
as Colonel of the First Virginia Regiment. And this placed him
in command also of the Second Virginia Regiment, whose actual tactical leader was the experienced Colonel Woodward.
Patrick Henry, however, had never had any military experience. Therefore, some of the other political leaders feared to
trust him with actual military command of the attack they were
planning to mount against the forces of Dunmore.

It was a tricky political situation. Patrick Henry was the
hero of the militia units, and of the whole Colony. Many of the
men had enlisted specifically to serve under him. Great dis-
content would arise if he were slighted, and not given opportu-
nity to exercise the command to which he'd been voted by the
House of Burgesses. But the Committee of Safety of the Colony determined that the more experienced Colonel Woodward
should actually lead the attack against Dunmore. Accord-
ingly, it was the Second Regiment which was ordered to
march to the defense of the towns south of the James River.

Colonel Woodward marched the regiment to Jamestown itself, planning to ferry his men across the river and thus save
them a long trek back north and around the head of the river.
But when he and his force arrived in Jamestown, they found
the British warship, *H.M.S. King's Otter*, cruising back and
forth in the river. Her guns would blow to pieces the small
boats in which the Virginians had planned to ferry their men
across!

"We'll have to march back to the head of the river," he told
his officers. "We can't cross with that ship there—we'd be
slaughtered by their ship's guns!"

The officers agreed. Turning, they redirected their marching columns back upriver to Sandy River. Here they found a small British vessel—lacking naval cannons—guarding that crossing. The militiamen quickly spread out along the shore, and at Woodward's command fired such a devastating volley that the ship beat a hasty retreat down river. The Virginians untied the small boats along the shore and dock, piled in, and were ferried across. Once on the other shore, they marched rapidly toward the south and east, eager to protect that area from Dunmore's dreaded raids.

But would the Second Regiment arrive in time to stop Dummore's further destruction of farms and supplies?

CHAPTER SIX

Capture the Girl!

Back in Williamsburg, Stephen and John had failed to report to Stephen's father the fact that they'd witnessed the arrest of Jed and his friends. For several days, they'd rushed off on errands in other parts of the town, hoping to avoid having to tell Mr. Bancroft of the danger to which he was now exposed with the arrest of Jed.

But a servant of Stephen's father found them at Mr. Bancroft's store later this morning. He told them that Mr. Bancroft wanted them to report to him at once at his house. Now, the young men were hurrying to comply.

"Not too fast!" Stephen cautioned, as he and John crossed another street on the way to Stephen's home. "We don't want anyone to notice us, and if you don't slow down they will!"

John's thin face could not conceal his fear. "But those militiamen *saw* us the other day when Jed got beaten up! I *know* they did! And that group marching behind us could be the same men! They're just about to catch up with us! We can't afford to let them recognize us!"

"They *may* have seen us," Stephen replied firmly, "and they may not have seen us. But no one recognized us—most of the militia who're in town now aren't from Williamsburg, remember. And they're not following—I sneaked a look a minute ago. No one's following us, so don't panic."

Thus encouraged, John twisted his head to look behind—
and promptly stumbled on a brick in the road, sprawling
face-down to the ground! Cursing, he jumped to his feet and
brushed the dust from his clothes.

"What a fool!" Stephen snapped, angered now. "That's the
way to attract attention!" He glanced fearfully to each side,
wondering if John's fall had caused any one to notice them.
But apparently it had not; the people he saw were going about
their own business, and no one seemed to be bothered with the
two hurrying youths.

They turned left, heading north now, and walked past a
number of houses before reaching Stephen's home. The long
white frame house with dormer windows reflected the wealth
and business success of Stephen's father, Mr. Bancroft, and
Stephen never failed to swell with pride as he compared his
own home to the smaller ones to either side. The two unlatched
the low gate in the picket fence, and walked up the path to the
steps that led to the porch.

"Where's Father?" Stephen asked the first servant he found
in the wide high-ceilinged hall.

"He's in his office, Master Stephen."

John followed the arrogant youth as he hurried through the
house and out the back door. Stephen rushed to the small-scale
house that served his father as his office in Williamsburg, and
soon he and John were explaining what they had seen around
the militia camp the past several days.

"There's over a thousand men there, Father!" Stephen said.
"We asked several men about their companies yesterday, and
again today, and we put it all together as more than a thousand
men."

"Men? You call them 'men'? I call them 'Rabble!'" his father snorted. Mr. Bancroft was a large man, tall like his son, but very much overweight. His portly frame was encased as usual in very expensive clothes. His satin breeches and long coat were topped by his red face and magnificent white-powdered wig. Shrewd gray eyes peered from under bushy white eyebrows as he questioned the two young men.

"Did you get any names?" he asked. "Company commanders, and the counties they came from?"

"Yes, Father," Stephen replied with a confident smile. "We did. I've got a list right here." He pulled a folded parchment from his pocket and handed this to his father. "The men have no idea of military secrecy! They love to talk, especially about themselves and their military prowess. You'd think they were real soldiers!"

"Rabble!" his father snorted again, unfolding the parchment and scanning his son's information with great interest. "They won't know what soldiers are 'til they face British Regulars. Then they'll scatter like chicken fleeing a hungry fox!"

"Sit down, you two," he said, waving them to chairs. He remained standing as he packed his long clay pipe and prepared to light.

"I'm immensely pleased!" Mr. Bancroft said, as smoke puffed from the lighted pipe. "You two have done well. No trouble, then?"

Stephen's smile was wiped from his face. "Actually, Father, there was."

His father straightened quickly. "What happened?"

"Well, several days ago, Jed Marks. . ." Stephen began, until his father interrupted him.

"Did that idiot make a fool of himself again?" he asked. "I told him firmly to be quiet, to attract no attention to himself, to pretend to be a Patriot and mingle with the militia in their camp by the college and learn all he could! What did he do this time?"

John spoke then. "Sir, you know how he hates that boy Andrew Hendricks. Jed can't stand the fact that the daughter of Andrew's partner won't even look at him. He thinks she's taken a shine to Andrew—and Jed can't stand that. So when he saw Andrew and that girl, and Andrew's sister, bringing a wagon of supplies to the militia camp, he caused trouble."

Horrified, Mr. Bancroft listened as the two told of Jed's attempt to stampede the wagon—right in front of a number of militiamen.

"What?" Mr. Bancroft asked incredulously. "Of all the stupid things to do! Those girls might have been hurt! What got into the man?"

"He was laughing," Stephen said, "laughing as he ran alongside the horses, shouting in their ears, trying to spook them all the way to Richmond it seemed like."

"Then Jed and his men rushed Andrew," Archer said. "Andrew had pulled the horses to a stop, and was helping the girls get down, when Jed and his men attacked him."

"In front of the militiamen?" Mr. Bancroft asked again. He was appalled at Jed's stupidity.

"Yes, sir. I don't think Jed even saw the militiamen. He just saw Andrew and those girls. He was having fun giving them a scare on a runaway wagon. But when Andrew got the horses under control—you should have seen him handle those horses, Father!—Jed and the others rushed him."

"What happened?"

Stephen fell silent. He hated to tell his father of Andrew's fighting skill.

John noticed Stephen's silence, and realized that Mr. Bancroft wanted an answer.

"Andrew can fight, Mr. Bancroft," John said. He licked his lips nervously at the memory of Andrew's skill, and went on to explain. "He knocked the first man down, then knocked Jed down too. He hurt 'em bad. The third man was afraid to attack him, and tried to run away. But the militiamen caught him. Those men were furious that Jed and his friends had put those girls in danger on a runaway wagon. They took all three of 'em to the gaol. They had to help Jed walk—he acted like Andrew had broken his ribs!"

"Gaol!" Mr. Bancroft exclaimed. "But that means they might come question me again! They know Jed has worked for me! Why didn't you fools tell me this at once? This is a calamity!"

He stormed back and forth in the room, raging at the danger Jed and his foolish friends may have caused, raging also at his son's failure to tell him this news the day it happened.

"We barely escaped gaol ourselves when the Patriots found those messages we'd prepared for Governor Dunmore! Now, if they connect Jed's actions to me again, we'll all be in jeopardy!"

"Father, Andrew and those girls have got to be stopped somehow," Stephen interjected. "You *know* that they're spies for the Patriots!"

"I *told* the Governor that," his father said. "But he said we can't do anything about girls. And that they probably just stumbled on the information they got. They're not important, he said. Neither is that boy, or his friend."

"But now Jed's in gaol, and we are again in danger, Father!" Stephen said, rising. "Those boys and girls keep threatening us with complete ruin! Something's *got* to be done about them!"

"I agree!" his father said. "Something's got to be done. I'll think about it. But, right now, we've got to save ourselves from the danger that fool Jed's gotten us in! We've got to plan what we should do about Jed's being in gaol! And what we'll do if those Patriots connect him to me again!"

He paced nervously back and forth in the room, muttering to himself. Finally he stopped and faced them. "You two get out of town at once!" he said. "You've got to get away from here, in case Capt. Innes comes to question you. You said that some of those militiamen saw you watching Andrew fight Jed? Then you've got to leave at once! Mount up, and ride to the farm. Stay there until I send for you."

"What will you do, Father?" Stephen said as he rose.

"I'll go to see Mr. Carter Nicholas right away," he said. "Mr. Nicholas hates this rebellion. He doesn't want a war. But he's angered at the government in London, too, as well as with Governor Dunmore. He wants to keep me and the men who think as I do pacified. He believes our leaders can outmaneuver the rebels so that we can avoid conflict."

Mr. Bancroft stood in thought for a moment. "Mr. Nicholas hopes that there won't be conflict—but I think he's wrong. And yet, as long as he thinks that way, he's useful to us, because he wants to hold back the more violent rebels. I'll go to him, just for a visit, and talk about how we can all work together to keep Virginia from war."

"But what if the Patriots come get you after they've questioned Jed, Mr. Bancroft" John asked.

"I'll tell them I have nothing more to do with that rascal!" Mr. Bancroft snapped. "That I sent him packing weeks ago! Mr. Nicholas will vouch for me. I'll weather this, I'm sure. But what a fool Jed is to jeopardize us all because of his hate for that Hendricks boy!"

Mr. Bancroft turned and closed the books he'd been studying. "You men get going! I'll stay in town. If Capt. Innes and the other leaders ask about you, I'll tell them you're at the plantation. Get out there, start working with the accounts, spread papers all over the office, make it look like you've been there all day, and tell the servants to back you up!"

The two hurried from the office and into the yard, Stephen yelling for servants to saddle their horses. Mr. Bancroft closed his account books, and called for his own horse. Mounting with difficulty because of his bulk, he turned his horse toward the home of Mr. Nicholas. As he rode, his mind was tormented with worry about Jed and his men being in gaol.

How much will Jed tell them if Capt. Innes really threatens him? he asked himself. *What a fool I was to use a fool to work for me!* He thought of Jed's idiocy in letting his hate for Andrew cause him to forget all caution, and thus endanger them all.

Then Bancroft thought of his own hate for Virginia's Patriots. This is what had caused him to forget his own prudence and hire Jed to serve as a spy for the Governor.

Hate blinds us all, he concluded grimly. He hoped he hadn't learned this lesson too late.

As he dismounted before the home of Mr. Nicholas, he came to another conclusion. *Stephen's right: We've got to capture Andrew, or one of those girls. They're just too involved in the Patriot activities! Whenever they appear, disaster happens to the Governor's cause! We've got to capture one of them and find out what they know and how they're being used by the rebels!*

He thought about it some more, then came to a conclusion. *"We'll capture that Edwards girl!"*

CHAPTER SEVEN

Find the Second Regiment!

The courier galloped madly along the street, dust flying from his horse's heels, until he came to Nelson Edward's house. Hauling the foaming mount to a stop, the rider leaped from the saddle, threw the reins hastily around the rail before the gate, burst through this and rushed toward the house. Sprinting up the steps, he ground to a halt and pounded on the door.

Sarah opened the door, and was surprised when the man thrust a letter into her hand.

"Give this to your father!" he said urgently. "Tell him to read it and send it to the Second Regiment! At once!"

Before the startled girl could reply, the messenger dashed down the steps, ran through the gate, untied his mount and vaulted into the saddle. Spurring the horse into a gallop, he raced back the way he had come, pursued by a pack of madly barking dogs.

"Who was that, Sarah?" her mother asked, coming into the hall from the kitchen.

"I don't know, Mother" Sarah replied. "He's a messenger and he was in a terrible hurry! He gave me this letter and said to give it to Father. Then he said Father must send it to the Second Regiment at once! What does that mean?"

"Heaven knows!" her mother replied. "But I suppose your father will. Take it to him right away."

"Yes, Mother," the girl replied. She moved swiftly through the hall to the kitchen, stepped out the door, down the steps, and hurried toward the one storey building her father and Mr. Hendricks used for their office. She knocked on the door, and was told, "Come in."

Entering, she found her father and Mr. Hendricks standing by the desk in conversation. Both men smiled when she entered.

"Father, a man galloped up to the house with this letter and said for you to read this and then send it to the Second Regiment right away!" She handed him the letter.

Mr. Hendricks glanced quickly at Nelson Edwards. "Well, we told Capt. Innes we'd provide a courier for him, but we didn't think he'd need one so fast!"

"We didn't," Edwards agreed. Untying the black ribbon that was wrapped around the thick folded paper, he opened the letter and read it swiftly.

His face grew stern. "This news is bad, William. Dunmore's been reinforced again, from the Fourteenth British Regiment in Florida! Our Committee of Safety wants to alert Colonel Woodward at once—he's facing more redcoats than he expected! And there's more bad news: Dunmore's forces defeated our militia at Kemp's landing. Most of our men have been scattered! Now there's no Patriot militia in that area to oppose him but the Second Regiment. Colonel Woodward could be marching into a trap, and he's got to be warned!"

Edwards glanced up from the letter with its dire news. "They need a messenger right away."

"Your boy's still in the Valley, Nelson," Hendricks said. "I'll send Andrew." He looked again at Sarah. "Sarah, would you please call him for me? He's in the barn loading wagons."

"Yes, sir," she said.

Sarah left the office and hurried across the yard toward the barn. Beside it, two large freight wagons were parked, their teams already hitched. These were about to be taken to the river where their loads would be transferred to the schooner. The large double-doors of the building were opened, and Sarah could see Andrew and Wilbur rolling barrels up the ramp and into the wagon.

Wilbur saw her first. A friendly giant of a man, he served as foreman for her father and Mr. Hendricks. Wilbur's broad face broke into a big smile as she approached. "Hello, Sarah! Want to help us roll these barrels up the ramp and into the wagon?"

"No, thank you!" she replied with a laugh. "They might roll back on me—then Father would put you and Andrew in the stocks!"

Wilbur and Andrew both laughed at this.

"Andrew," Sarah said, "Father asked you to come to the office. He wants you to take a message for Capt. Innes."

"Yes, indeed!" Andrew said, breaking into a huge smile. He turned to Wilbur and tried to look disappointed. "Wilbur, it grieves me to leave you with all this work—but, of course, I have no choice. You heard what she said!"

"I bet it grieves you!" Wilbur laughed. "Go ahead; I'll get Sam to help me finish loading."

Andrew jumped down from the wagon and hurried with Sarah toward the house. "What did your father tell you about this?" he asked eagerly.

"He didn't tell me anything," she said. "But, goodness, Andrew! Slow down—you're walking too fast! A messenger just galloped up to the house and gave me this, and said for Father to send it to the Second Regiment right away. What does that mean, Andrew? Where's the Second Regiment?"

"That's the Regiment Colonel Woodward commands," Andrew replied, his voice unable to hide his excitement. "It's been sent south and east, down past Hampton, to stop Governor Dunmore's raids against the towns and homes there. The other Regiment, under Colonel Patrick Henry, stayed here to guard Williamsburg."

"Then I suspect they'll send you with this message. You won't get drawn into any fighting, will you?" she asked anxiously.

"I'm sure I won't," he replied. "But maybe Father will ask me to take them the message. I wonder what it says?"

"Can't they send someone else?" she asked. Governor Dunmore had caused a lot of trouble in that part of Virginia with his raids, they'd heard, and now, with more British soldiers to reinforce him, he'd be even more dangerous.

"Not anyone as reliable as me!" he said with a straight face, hoping to make her laugh.

"I wish you and Nathan weren't sent on these trips, Andrew," she said very seriously.

"Don't worry," he replied, both flustered and pleased at her concern, "our fathers aren't sending us into danger."

"That's what they told us when they sent you to New York with the schooner last June," she reminded him. "But you know what happened then!"

He did indeed. He and Nathan had ended up in the middle of the battle for Bunker Hill, and had been fortunate to escape the encircling British redcoats! And just a couple of weeks ago, Andrew had ridden into a British patrol alone and barely escaped after a fight with a British officer.

"Don't worry, Sarah," he said, patting her shoulder as they came to the door of their fathers' office. "I'll just take the message for Captain Innes—if father asks me, that is. I won't attack Governor Dunmore's troops!"

Once inside the office, William Hendricks lost no time in telling Andrew of his mission.

"With our militia units scattered, and Governor Dunmore reinforced," his father concluded, "Colonel Woodward and the Second Regiment have got to beware they don't march into a trap!"

Nelson Edwards folded and retied the letter, then handed this to Andrew. "Your father's volunteered you again, Andrew," he said with a smile. "Take this to Colonel Woodward."

"Come back as soon as Colonel Woodward can release you, Andrew," his father said. "But now, ride at once to Sandy Point. Our scouts reported yesterday that the British ship is no longer blocking the river there. Take the ferry across. Then ride fast toward Suffolk, and find the Second Regiment and

Colonel Woodward. He's got to know the danger he's in, now
that Dummore's been reinforced!"

Half an hour later—it was still nine in the morning this cold
day—Andrew trotted his horse out of Williamsburg, heading
toward Sandy Point. Tied behind his saddle in a rolled blanket
was his food, canteen, and camping gear. His long cloak covered his thick buckskin shirt and legging, keeping him warm.
The polished stock of his long rifle protruded from its case in
front of his knee. Knife and tomahawk were in his belt. *Dusty*
trotted briskly, eager to break into a run; Andrew kept him under tight rein.

Shortly after leaving town, Andrew passed a company of
militia marching the same way as he was. He waved, and their
leader waved back. Periodically, he passed wagons and riders
coming from the other direction. When he arrived at the ferry
landing, he was pleased to see the boat about to dock on his
side of the river; he was able to cross within half-an-hour of its
landing. Once across the river, he put the stallion into a run,
anxious to cover as much distance as he could before dark.

He made good time that afternoon, and stopped at a farmhouse as dusk was falling. The friendly family invited him to
share their evening meal with them, then spend the night in
their barn. They too had news of Governor Dunmore's doings
—none of it good.

"The Governor's persuaded a lot of people in Norfolk and
Portsmouth to change their loyalty back to the Crown," the
farmer told him grimly. "Hundreds of men have sworn their
allegiance, in fact. It's looking bad for the Patriot cause now!"

"What about our militia units?" Andrew asked in surprise.

"Dunmore's scattered 'em," the farmer told him. "Others went over to the Governor. They think he's going to win. And he will, too, if he keeps up his raids, and if people see that the Patriots can't stop him!"

Andrew went to bed with an anxious heart. But he slept soundly, and rose very early the next morning. After downing a hasty breakfast with the family, he saddled up, and headed at a fast pace along the road that took him toward Suffolk.

Around ten that morning he saw a rider galloping toward him from the south. Waving him to a halt, Andrew recognized the man as one of Captain Innes's messengers. The rider recognized Andrew as well. Andrew asked him if he knew the whereabouts of Colonel Woodward and the Second Regiment.

"I sure do!" the man replied, glad to give his horse a respite. "He's sent me back to Williamsburg with a message for the Committee of Safety. He wants them to know that the Governor has declared the whole State to be in rebellion—that means that any man that doesn't rally to him and the King's cause is a traitor to be tried and hung!"

Andrew was stunned by this. "But that'll make everybody have to decide right now!" he said. "Lots of people haven't decided yet—they need to see that we can beat the Governor before they're willing to fight against him. We've got to have more time to show them we can whip 'em!"

"We'd *like* more time," the messenger said grimly. "But we don't have it! Everyone in Virginia is now either a traitor or a loyal supporter of the King—that's what the Governor's proclamation means! We just don't know what this will do to the people who haven't made up their minds to join us yet. Colonel Woodward's worried bad about this."

Then they parted. Andrew put *Dusty* into a run for half-a-mile before slowing him to a trot. He alternated his pace throughout the morning, dismounting and resting the horse periodically, wanting to make the best time he could without wearing out his mount.

CHAPTER EIGHT

An Arrow Aimed at Virginia!

A couple of days later, dusk fell on a weary and travel-stained Andrew as he returned at last to Williamsburg. Reaching his home, he rode into the back yard and dismounted at the barn. He opened the wide door and led his tired mount inside. He had just lit a lantern, and had begun to unsaddle the animal, when suddenly he heard a rush of feet behind him. Turning quickly, he saw Sarah hurry into the barn.

"Andrew!" she cried, coming to a stop just before him. "Did you just ride in!" Her dark hair fell on the collar of her gray wool dress, her cheeks were red with the cold, and her eyes were shining with pleasure at his return.

Andrew's tired face broke into a smile. "You're going to freeze without your cloak!" he said, whipping his own cloak from his shoulders and throwing it around her. "Yes, I just rode in this minute. I brought back messages for Captain Innes, then came straight home. How'd you know I'd gotten back?"

"Oh, I just happened to look out the kitchen window and over at the barn; that's how I saw you ride up." She smiled her thanks for the cloak, and didn't mention that she'd been looking out the kitchen window all that afternoon, whenever she'd had the chance, wondering when he'd return. Quickly she changed the subject and began to ask a torrent of questions about his trip.

"Did you find the Second Regiment? And did you see Colonel Woodward? And did you see any Tories? Or British soldiers? Has there been fighting yet? Did more of our militia switch sides and join the British? Andrew—tell me the truth, now!—were you in any danger? And you won't have to go back, will you?"

"Goodness, Sarah!" he exclaimed when she finished, as he began to rub down the horse with an old piece of blanket. "How do girls think of so many things to ask at once?"

"Andrew, why are boys so difficult to talk to? They don't want to tell you *anything!* Now, answer my questions!"

"But which ones?" he said with a grin.

"All of them!" she replied, stamping her foot. "Start with the first—did you find the Second Regiment? And did you see Colonel Woodward? And was there any fighting with the British? And is it true that a lot of Virginia militiamen are switching sides and joining the British? We've heard the most awful rumors!"

"I did find the Second Regiment," he said. "And the Colonel was sure glad to get the message I gave him. And it is true that a lot of militia left the Patriots and joined the British—that was part of the message I took Colonel Woodward. He didn't know so many of our militia had gone over to Governor Dunmore. So he gave orders to march the regiment to a safer camping place, and put out more scouts, so the Governor's troops couldn't catch them by surprise."

"Did any British shoot at you?" she asked anxiously.

"Now, Sarah, I *told* you I wouldn't get *near* any British!"

"You *told* me that before," she replied, "but you didn't keep your word! Please answer me, Andrew." She followed closely as he moved around to the other side of his horse and toweled the tired animal.

"No, I didn't even *see* any British, thank the Lord!" he replied. "I just tracked down the Second Regiment and gave the Colonel the message. Then I visited with Matthew Anderson while the Colonel met with his officers. He wrote a letter for me to take back to the Committee of Safety in Williamsburg. So I came straight back. I spent last night in a farmer's barn." Wearily he hung his saddle and bridle up on their pegs. "Man, am I tired!"

He's grown these past months, Sarah thought to herself, noticing his broad shoulders as he hung up the saddle.

Andrew *had* grown that year, taller and wider, and his shoulders and arms had thickened with the constant work in his father's shipping business.

Andrew poured feed into a leather bucket, poured water as well, led the horse into the stall, and shut the gate. Picking up his long rifle and pack, he extinguished the lantern. Sarah walked beside him as he went outside and closed the wide door behind them. It was almost dark, now. Lights shone merrily from his own home, and from the Edwards' house next door.

"I'll walk you home," he said. "Tell me what kinds of trouble you and Rachel got into while I was gone."

"Well," she replied, with a very straight face, "first we sneaked into the Powder Magazine the night you left town and blew it up. That was fun! Then, the very next day, we set fire to the College—you should have seen those militiamen run from their camp like a bunch of ants from an anthill! We just laughed and laughed! Then we climbed up on the windmill and sawed off all its arms. After that, we. . ."

"All right!" he conceded with a grin. "So you saw more action than I did!"

"Of course," she replied. "That's why you shouldn't leave us like that. You're supposed to stay home and keep us safe and out of trouble. I'm going to have to tell your father that you neglected your duty to your own sister—and to me, her friend!—and that he shouldn't let you go away any more!"

"Why don't you tell him instead to let you ride with me; then I could see that you behaved yourself? I'd keep you from getting into all that trouble!" he said with a smile.

She laughed happily at the ridiculous thought. "I don't think either of our fathers would let me ride to the army with you!" she said. "Remember, they won't let me and Rachel go near the militia camp at the College anymore!"

"Well, they're right about that!" he said. His face became grave as he thought of the dangerous stunt Jed and his friends had pulled when they caused the horses of the wagon to break into a gallop. Thinking of that made him ask, "Has anyone seen Jed?"

"No, thank heavens!" she exclaimed gratefully. "After all the punishment he got in the stocks, no one's seen him—or his friends, either! They've just vanished! They got lots of dirt clods thrown at their faces every day! And you'd broken Jed's ribs, and the nose of that big man! They were miserable!" She shuddered at the malignancy of those villains, and prayed they'd never come into their lives again. But she had a strange sense that she not seen the last of Jed.ˑ

"Well, they deserved a lot more than that," he said quietly.

"Everybody says how fine you were to beat them up like you did, Andrew," she said. "Everyone admires you for that! I do too! Rachel and I told everyone about it!"

He was thankful that the dark kept her from seeing how red his face became with her generous praise. He couldn't think of anything to say—so he didn't say anything.

They approached the back porch of the Edwards home. "Come in, and I'll give you some hot chocolate," she said brightly.

"Let me go tell my family I'm home," he replied, "then I'll come right back."

"Tell them we want to hear all about your trip," she urged, as they walked side by side up the steps. "Bring Rachel with you."

"I'll try!" he said, opening the door for her.

She walked in, smiling up at him, and he closed the door after her. His pace quickened as he walked down the steps and turned toward his own house. For some reason, he didn't feel so tired now. He ran up his own back steps and went into the kitchen—to a boisterous welcome from his family.

A short while later, Andrew went back to the Edwards' house, accompanied by his father and mother and Rachel. Andrew's older sister, Laura, remained home with little Benjamin. Soon the two families were seated comfortably in the Edwards' large kitchen, drinking hot chocolate. They all asked Andrew question after question about his trip. Candles on pewter sconces on the wall threw their beams through their glass chimneys, casting a friendly light over the cheerful room.

Mrs. Edwards and Sarah and Rachel were busy passing out thick pieces of warm pie from the oven. The younger children were already asleep in their room. And Sarah's brother Nathan was still absent with a wagon load of goods their fathers had sent to Richmond.

William Hendricks and Nelson Edwards were very concerned about the success of Governor Dunmore in defeating the Virginia militia, and in actually recruiting some hundreds of them into his own army.

"So the militiamen took the oath to fight for the King!" Nelson Edwards said quietly. He sat at the end of the table, sipping his chocolate.

"Yes, sir, a hundred of 'em did on the 16th," Andrew replied. "Those were men who'd started to fight Dunmore's troops, then quit. And later the same day, more than two hundred militiamen in Norfolk switched sides and swore to fight for the King. The town leaders gave a great feast for them all, and now they're fortifying the town so the Patriots can't take it back!"

"Then Dunmore's army is growing," Andrew's father observed.

"Yes, sir, it is. But there's worse to come! After the Governor set up headquarters in Norfolk, and after those two hundred militiamen switched sides, a militia lieutenant colonel named Ellegood led six hundred Norfolk militia to join the Crown! The Governor made him Colonel and called his unit the Queen's Own Loyal Regiment! The Governor's getting more and more men all the time from that part of Virginia. And if the British Government sends him more troops and ships. . ."

"They'll split the American colonies in two," Nelson Edwards interjected. "Right in two! And that will stop Virginia from sending men to George Washington's army around Boston."

"That will stop Virginia from sending him supplies also," William Hendricks said gravely. "We're sending an immense amount of food and military equipment to the Northern Army. We can't do that now, not with Dunmore on the loose! We need all our men and all our supplies right here in Virginia! Dunmore's building himself a real army."

"Dunmore's an arrow aimed at the heart of the colonies, then," Andrew's mother observed soberly.

"That's right, Carolyn," her husband agreed. "That's well put—he's an arrow aimed at the heart of the colonies."

"Can't our militia do anything to stop him?" Sarah asked.

"They mean to try," Andrew said. "Colonel Woodward's waiting for some reinforcements from North Carolina. He wants them to block food supplies from getting to Governor Dunmore's forces in Norfolk. And he wants cannon, to attack a fort the British built on a place called Great Bridge. But Colonel Woodward's men need blankets, and gunpowder, and lead for bullets. They're real short of all kinds of supplies."

Andrew paused a moment, wondering if he should tell them something else he'd heard from a number of the militiamen. He decided he would. "Matthew Anderson says that Colonel

Woodward's a mighty cautious man; he isn't moving to attack as fast as some of the officers and men want him to."

Nelson Edwards and William Hendricks exchanged glances. Edwards spoke first. "Well, I imagine he's got to be sure his troops are ready before he attacks. Did Captain Innes say he wanted you to ride for him again, Andrew?"

"No, sir, not exactly. He just asked if I'd be able to ride if the Committee of Safety needed me to take another message to the Second Regiment."

"What did you tell him?" Sarah asked quickly.

He looked across the table at her anxious eyes. Reluctantly, he replied: "I told him I would if Father agreed."

Suddenly the fatigue from the long days in the saddle came over Andrew like a flood. He felt his eyes closing, and struggled to keep awake.

"Well, I'd sure rather have you taking messages to Colonel Woodward than marching in those marshes with the Second Regiment!" her mother said firmly. Then she noticed Andrew's head nodding.

"Goodness, William!" she exclaimed, rising quickly. "This boy's about to fall asleep! Let's get him home at once!"

"You go ahead, Carolyn," her husband replied. "Take him and Rachael with you. I'll come in a few minutes."

Andrew rose slowly from the chair, smiling wearily at Sarah. "Thanks for welcoming me back," he said.

She smiled. "Thank you for walking me home."

Andrew stood for a moment looking at her. Then he realized suddenly that everyone in the room was smiling at him. His face flamed, and he turned hastily and walked toward the door. His mother and Rachel thanked Sarah and her mother for the hot chocolate and pie, then followed Andrew out of the house. Mrs. Edwards and Sarah retired, leaving Edward Nelson and William Hendricks alone.

The two men looked gravely at each other.

Nelson Edwards broke the silence. "I think events in Virginia are building to a climax, William, and they're building more quickly than are our military preparations. No one thought Dunmore would have such success."

"I'm afraid that you're right," Hendricks replied. "Our leaders certainly can't allow Dunmore to keep adding militia units to his army—soon he'll be too strong for us to attack. In fact, if he just holds Norfolk and Portsmouth for a while longer, the British Government's bound to send him enough reinforcements to make him impregnable to any attack our raw troops could mount against him. Surely the men in London see what an advantage he's given them, holding those two seaports!"

"I hope that they don't," Edwards replied, rising and walking to the fire. He took one of the iron tongs, fished out a glowing coal, and lit his long clay pipe.

"Remember," Edwards continued, "it takes months for news to get back and forth across the ocean. It's quite possible that London has no idea what an advantage Dunmore's won for them. The British leaders there might not know for a long time just how successful the Governor's been. If our forces can strike Dunmore now, before he gets any stronger, they might be able to stop his buildup before it becomes too formidable."

"Let's pray that they'll do just that," Hendricks said, rising from his chair. "I'll see Captain Innes in the morning, then."

"He's certainly free to use Andrew to take messages from the Committee to the Second Regiment. I'm glad the boy can help."

Hendricks stood for a moment in thought. Then he glanced at his friend. "That was an apt description Carolyn gave of Dunmore—"an arrow aimed at the heart of the colonies!"

Nelson Edwards nodded. "An arrow aimed at Virginia, certainly! Let's pray that the Second Regiment can blunt that arrow before it hits again," he said.

CHAPTER NINE

Ride Fast! Stop for No One!

Two days later, Andrew and his father rode from their home to meet Captain Innes at the Raleigh Tavern. They found the commander of the Williamsburg Volunteer Company standing beside his tethered horse in front of the tavern, a worried frown on his weathered face. He brightened when they rode up, glanced around to see if anyone was near, and quickly suggested that they change their place of meeting.

"The Raleigh's got too many visitors today," he said gravely, "and some of 'em are strangers. Let's go over to Shield's. I don't want any spies of the Governor to hear our conversation."

"Fine," William Hendricks agreed, turning his horse. Captain Innes stepped into the saddle and the three rode across the street, then east, past the King's Arms Tavern, past John Coke's office, to Shield's Tavern. Here they halted, and dismounted.

None of them noticed the two men who walked casually out of the Raleigh Tavern and crossed the street after them. The men were both dressed in the long hunting shirts of the militia, with knives and tomahawks in their belts. Broad black-brimmed hats were pulled low over their eyes. Untying their horses from the rail, the two mounted swiftly and followed Captain Innes and the Hendricks to Shield's Tavern.

Tying their horses to the rail in front of Shield's Tavern, Captain Innes, William Hendricks, and Andrew walked up the several steps and entered the center part of the long building. Once inside, they turned to their right, entered the room, and found a booth in the far back corner. Andrew had brought his long rifle with him, and as he sat down he propped this against the wall. Captain Innes took a seat facing the back wall, while Andrew and his father sat opposite him. William Hendricks was on the inside of the booth, next to the wall. Andrew, on the outside of the bench, had a view of most of the room.

The air was thick with the smell of fresh cooking and pipe-smoke. There were a number of men seated at the various tables, most of them deep in serious conversation. A servant came up and Andrew's father and Captain Innes asked for coffee. Andrew ordered hot cider.

The Captain reached across the table and handed Andrew a thick and worn brown leather case. "Here's a batch of letters for Colonel Woodward, Andrew. We appreciate your willingness to ride for us; our other couriers are gone already, and the Colonel's got to get these messages right away!"

Captain Innes glanced at Andrew's father. "Thank you, William, for lending us your son! We need him bad!"

"You're most welcome," Hendricks said, lighting up his long clay pipe. "Then the Committee of Safety thinks Colonel Woodward's regiment is strong enough to attack Dunmore's forces now?"

"The Committee thinks Colonel Woodward's regiment *has got* to attack Dunmore now!" the Captain said emphatically, lowering his voice but speaking with great emphasis. "Before Dunmore can persuade more Virginia militia units to switch sides and join him! Before the British Government sends him more reinforcements! Before it's too late! There are some who think Colonel Woodward's waited too long already!"

The two men who had followed them from the Raleigh Tavern came into the room then and paused at the doorway, searching the room with quick glances. Spotting Andrew in the back booth, the larger of the men quickly glanced away, as if looking for someone else.

"They're back there in the corner," he said out of the side of his mouth to the tough-looking stocky man beside him. "And there's an empty booth this side of 'em. I'll wander over there. You join me in a minute. This is a stroke of luck—we'll be able to hear what they say!"

The stocky man grunted, turned back, and walked into the other room. The big man walked casually toward the room on the right, then stopped at the door, changed course, and stepped quietly to the booth just behind the one where the Captain and the Hendricks were seated. He kept his eyes on the floor, hoping that Andrew wouldn't notice him.

But Andrew *had* noticed the two as they'd entered. He'd seen them separate, seen the taller man look at him a brief moment, then shift his eyes quickly away, then walk to the adjoining booth and sit down! Once the tall man sat down, however, Andrew was unable to see him—the high wooden partition that separated the booths hid him from his view. But Andrew knew that the man was there.

That man sat there on purpose! Andrew thought to himself, fully alert now. He wondered if he should warn Captain Innes and his father. But just then Captain Innes began speaking.

The Captain's voice was low; Andrew reasoned that maybe he couldn't be overheard by the man in the next booth.

Andrew was wrong.

"We've just learned that Dunmore's got almost two hundred redcoats from the Fourteenth Regiment," Captain Innes said quietly, as he leaned across the table. "And he's got more than a thousand Tories and militiamen! He's fortifying Norfolk for a garrison of at least five thousand men, and making gun ports for twenty cannon! Two thirds of the folk in Norfolk and Portsmouth have declared for the King already. His force is growing faster than ours!"

"The Governor's got more than a thousand men?" William Hendricks asked, his eyes widening. "Are you sure of that, James? That means that the British could control our coast already!"

"More than a thousand," Captain Innes insisted. "It's that bad. And if the British Government reinforces Dunmore soon, Virginia has no hope of dislodging him—and that will end our support of General Washington and the army surrounding the British at Boston! We won't be able to send anything out of the Colony to the northern army—not supplies, not fighting men, not anything! We'll need everything here to defend ourselves! So Colonel Woodward's *got* to attack Dunmore! He can't wait any longer."

The Captain spoke quietly at first, but his voice rose as he continued, and the tall man in the next booth heard almost everything that he said. One of the servants approached his table, but he waved him away. "Later," he said quietly. He didn't want to call any more attention to himself, and thus cause Captain Innes to lower his voice.

"Does Colonel Woodward not get the same news you get here, James? Do we know any more than he does already?" William Hendricks asked.

Captain Innes shook his head. "The river's between him and Norfolk, remember. We get horsemen with messages all the time. We probably get lots of information quicker than he does. But there's another thing. The Colonel doesn't have the latest information about the North Carolina militia units that are marching to join him, because we just got that information by schooner! That's why we've got to get a message to him right away. Because those North Carolina men want to join with the Virginia Second Regiment to crush Dunmore between them. Before Dunmore gets wind of their coming!"

Captain Innes turned his steady gaze on Andrew. "That's where you come in, Andrew. This message you're taking to the Colonel tells how many men the North Carolinians have got, who their leaders are, the roads they're taking, and when they expect to join Colonel Woodward."

William Hendricks glanced quickly at his son. Andrew's eyes had grown wide at the significance of the message the Committee of Safety was entrusting to him. Somehow, Andrew forgot about the man in the next booth.

"Then Andrew had better ride out right away, James," William Hendricks said.

"He'd better ride out right away," the Captain agreed. He reached into his pocket and handed over a small leather pouch. "Here's some coin for the tavern and for food for you and your horse, Andrew."

"Does anyone else beside the Committee members know the messages Andrew will be carrying?" William asked. "Is there any danger that Dunmore's men will try to intercept him?" His gray eyes looked keenly at the captain.

Just then the stocky man entered the room, walked quietly up to the next booth, and sat down.

Captain Innes started to answer William Hendrick's question, then hesitated. He'd just heard the man walk up behind him, and sit down. Innes clamped his jaw shut.

Andrew had seen the man walk in, spot someone in the booth, and walk casually over. He had a sudden sense of alarm—*Why were those men crossing the room to sit right by us?* he asked himself.

There are other empty booths and tables in the room!

Captain Innes lowered his voice and answered Hendricks' question. "We don't think so, William. No one's supposed to know about this message from the North Carolinians, and no one but the Committee's supposed to know the orders Andrew's carrying to Colonel Woodward."

The Captain glanced sharply at Andrew. "But you stay alert, boy, and don't trust no one you don't know. This information's *got* to reach Colonel Woodward!"

The two men in the next booth looked keenly at each other. The tall one said very quietly. "We've heard enough. I'll cross the street and get our horses, and wait for you at the Raleigh. You take your time—don't follow them out at once. We don't want to arouse their suspicions. We know the road the boy's taking—he's heading for the ferry. He can't get away from us."

The stocky man grinned wickedly. "Ross, the Governor'll give us money for these messages," he whispered.

"He sure will, Sam," Ross replied, as he rose casually and walked out of the room. He moved with easy grace.

Andrew noticed the tall man leave. Again he started to mention the men to Captain Innes, but the Captain was speaking.

"Ride fast, Andrew! Stop for no one!"

Andrew looked solemnly at the Captain. He was beginning to feel weighed down with the responsibility he'd been given. This mission was of vital importance to Virginia and to its independence. He was conscious that his father, sitting beside him, had turned his head and was regarding him with his steady gaze.

Captain Innes leaned across the table and spoke with great earnestness, his eyes boring into Andrew's. He spoke slowly, measuring carefully each word. "Don't trust anyone, Andrew. Don't join anyone. Don't let anyone join you. Take these messages to the Second Regiment with all the speed you can."

"Yes, sir," Andrew replied.

Captain Innes sat back and breathed a sigh. "I'll feel better when you return and I know that Colonel Woodward has received this information. He and his regiment will be in terrible danger until they know what forces Governor Dunmore has marshaled against them. You've got to reach Woodward before Dunmore can trap him and his men, and before Dunmore can spoil the trap the North Carolinians are planning for *him*!"

Andrew nodded solemnly. Again he wondered if he should mention the man who was still sitting in the next booth, and the man who'd left and gone outside. Then he decided he wouldn't. *I've got no reason to suspect them*, he thought finally.

A quarter of an hour later, Andrew rode out of Williamsburg at a fast trot, heading for the ferry at Sandy Point. Again he rode his father's favorite mount, the big brown stallion named *Dusty*. The long rifle was in its deerskin scabbard just in front of his right leg, a big double-barreled pistol rode in a long leather holster in front of his left knee, and in his belt he carried a tomahawk and long knife. Behind his saddle were his blanket roll and camping gear. The leather pouch with its letters for Colonel Woodward was deep in the pocket of his long hunting shirt.

Periodically Andrew put *Dusty* into a run. The big horse was eager to gallop, but Andrew knew enough not to wear him out at the outset of their trip. Andrew loved this powerful animal; Dusty could run for a long time without tiring, and was unusually calm and reliable.

"He's a great horse to be riding if you get into a chase or a fight!" his father had assured him. Andrew hoped he wouldn't be getting into either.

Andrew, of course, could not see the two riders who rode out of town a bare ten minutes after he did. Had he seen them, he would have recognized them as the men who'd sat in the next booth in Shield's tavern. But Andrew would not have known who they were. Neither man was known in Williamsburg, in fact—which is why the Governor had sent them to Mr. Bancroft to serve as messengers.

The men's names were Ross and Sam; Ross was the bigger man, and the leader. When Mr. Bancroft had learned from his own spy that the Committee had vital news to send to Colonel

Woodward, he had ordered Ross and Sam to shadow Captain Innes and learn what they could from the Captain's conversation with the messenger.

"Intercept that rider, if you can!" he told them. "Capture those letters the Committee's sending to Colonel Woodward. Find out what the rebels plan to do!"

Ross and Sam had indeed found out what the rebels planned to do. But they meant also to catch the messenger and take his letters from him. To this end, they were galloping out of Williamsburg in rapid pursuit of Andrew.

"We'll let him get a long ways out of town," Ross called over to Sam, who's horse was running beside his own. "When we spot him, we'll make sure no one else is in sight. We'll ride up on either side, you grab his reins, I'll point a pistol at him, and we'll pull him into the woods and get those letters he's carrying for the Committee of Safety!"

"Man, have I got plans for spending the money the Governor will give us for this!" Sam called back over the pounding of their horses hooves.

Ross grinned wickedly. "So have I! The Governor will be bowled over when he hears about the North Carolina troops. He'll be able to strike the rebels one group at a time, and wipe 'em out in detail, before they can join forces! Not only that: these letters from the Patriots' Committee of Safety authorize Virginians to wage war against the Governor's British troops. That means Dunmore will have all the legal authority he needs to hang 'em all! They've signed their death warrants! We're bringing him a treasure, and he'd better pay us well for it—and I know he will! We'll get gold for this, Sam! Gold!"

The two men urged their horses to greater speed. "Let's close the distance, Sam!" Ross called.

Just two miles ahead of the riders, utterly unaware that he was being pursued, Andrew pulled Dusty back from his run and settled into an fast trot. The words of Captain Innes were ringing in his ears: "RIDE FAST! STOP FOR NO ONE!"

But I've got to rest Dusty between gallops, he thought prudently. In a few minutes he'd slow the stallion to a walk.

Some time later, Andrew realized that he was not far from the ferry. He decided to walk *Dusty* again for several hundred yards—but it wasn't an easy task holding the animal in. The big horse was restive, bursting with power, eager to break into a run.

"Just wait a moment!" Andrew laughed, pulling back on the reins and holding the eager horse in check. "You'll get plenty of chances to run this day! And the next day as well! Besides, we're not far from the ferry—there's no need to hurry!"

Dusty tossed his head, and pranced a bit, as if to tell the boy that he *wanted* to gallop all the way to the river! Birds chirped in the woods on either side of the road, and a bright sun shone down. Yet the day was cold.

Just then, Dusty pricked up his ears and turned his head. Andrew heard suddenly the sound of pounding hooves behind. Looking over his shoulder, he saw a pair of riders bent low over their saddles, ridding side by side around a curve in the road just a hundred yards behind, riding as if the devil were after them.

"What's their hurry?" Andrew asked his horse as he twisted backwards to watch. Then he recognized the riders.

Those men were in the tavern! They heard our talk. And they know about the messages I'm carrying to Colonel Woodward!

He kicked his heels into *Dusty's* ribs and threw himself low over the saddle as the startled stallion gathered his powerful muscles and burst into a run.

Angry shouts followed him as *Dusty* gathered speed and galloped down the rough road. Andrew heard a pistol fired, then another! The frustrated men behind had believed that they were close enough to frighten Andrew to a stop, and were furious that he had galloped away. Cursing, they jammed their pistols into the holsters at the front of the saddles, and pulled out their second guns.

Thoroughly alarmed now, Andrew realized that he was riding for his life. He reached into the long deerskin holster in front of his saddle and pulled out the big two barreled pistol. This was his father's favorite handgun, and he'd begun to lend it to Andrew when the Committee of Safety had started to use him as a courier.

"Two shots are better than one, Andrew," his father had told him. "You know how to use it if you need to."

Andrew did indeed know how to use it. His father had taken great pains to teach him. But he hadn't expected that he'd need it to defend himself against riders from Williamsburg!

We're really at war! he thought desperately to himself. *I can't seem to get used to it, but it's true.*

The road turned to the left. Andrew guided Dusty with the reins held in his left hand, and gripped the big pistol in his right. As he swept round the curve, he threw a glance behind.

Now that *Dusty* had gotten into his stride, his pursuers had fallen behind. But they were still coming!

They won't catch this horse! Andrew thought to himself. *But they'll trap me against the river if the ferry's not ready to go!*

Andrew's thoughts were bleak. It was not likely that the ferry would be just sitting there waiting for him when he galloped up. *Most likely, it'll be on the river! Maybe on the other side! Then how'll I get away? They'll ride up and trap me against the river!*

He bent low, letting *Dusty* tear along the ground, knowing that he had a lead on his pursuers. But he knew also that it would be of no avail should the men trap him at the riverside and catch him before he could get on the ferry and get out of firing range from the riverbank!

Behind him, Ross and Sam were cursing aloud their failure to stop Andrew before he could put that powerful stallion into a gallop.

"But we'll get him at the ferry!" Ross shouted over the pounding of their horses hooves. "He'll have to stop at the river!"

"What if he gets on the ferry before we get there?" Sam shouted back"

"Won't do him any good!" Ross gloated. "We'll draw our guns on the ferryman and make him stay at the dock, then we'll take that boy and his messages. Fast as that stallion is, he won't get there in time to get out of range of our guns—even if the ferry is ready to take him on! We'll get him, Sam! We'll get him!"

Ahead of the two pursuing riders, the big stallion galloped swiftly along the rough road, clods of dirt flying from his hooves. Bending low over the horse's neck, Andrew shoved the big two-barreled pistol back into its holster and gripped the reins with both hands.

It seemed to Andrew that *Dusty* increased his speed with every quarter mile that he ran, but he knew that probably wasn't true. Yet they flew along at a prodigious rate, drawing away from their two pursuers. Another bend in the road hid the men behind from Andrew's sight. The boy began to consider how he'd could escape the trap they'd close on him when he came to the river.

Even if the ferry's at the dock, it wouldn't have time to get into the middle of the river before those men would be shooting at me from the bank! Andrew thought. He leaned forward in the saddle as he guided the racing stallion along the treacherous road. *I've got to find a place to turn off. Maybe I can lose them in the forest, then get back to the ferry.*

Then another thought struck him. *If I can't lose 'em, I'll have to ambush 'em! But I can't let them keep me from taking these messages to the Second Regiment!*

The prospects were grim. But Andrew knew he had to try. Now the road straightened. Throwing a quick glance behind him, he saw the two men emerge from behind a cluster of trees nearly a third of a mile behind. But they were still in sight. They didn't have to catch him now; they just had to chase him to the river.

Looking ahead again, Andrew spotted suddenly a wagon trail leading away from the road to the left, just a hundred yards away. Knowing this was probably the best chance he would have to draw his pursuers away from the main road, Andrew began to haul back on the reins with all his might. With difficulty he slowed the stallion. Then, as they reached the wagon trail, he swerved *Dusty* into it. It was a rough trail, made worse by the low branches of trees that almost knocked Andrew from the saddle as the big horse tore through the thick underbrush. Andrew gripped the reins with both his hands as he guided the galloping stallion through the treacherous woods.

Andrew ducked under a thick branch that hung across the road. Then another limb hit his back as he bent low over the saddle. He pulled back on the reins again, frantically slowing the horse before they both collided into a branch that wouldn't give. There were enough evergreens to block his view ahead, and he knew that he'd better slow this mad pace.

Darting glances behind, he could not see the men who were chasing him. But he could hear their angry shouts as they too were struck by low tree branches. Suddenly the stallion leaped over a pile of branches directly before him, almost throwing Andrew out of the saddle! Andrew held the reins with one hand and thrust his other into the horse's thick mane. He just barely managed to keep his seat.

I've got to turn off and ambush them, he thought suddenly.

But where? He couldn't see far enough ahead through the branches to plan a trap. Slowing Dusty even more, praying that the men behind would not close the distance and shoot him in the back, Andrew looked frantically for a place to turn aside.

Then he saw it! To the left was a burnt piece of field perhaps fifty yards deep. *Lightning struck it maybe*, he thought, as he pulled *Dusty* into the field, barely managing to slow him enough to turn and ride back to the edge of the wood. He drew the big pistol again from the holster, and leaped to the ground, the reins gripped firmly in his left hand. Crouching, he waited for his pursuers to emerge from the narrow path.

"Steady, Steady!" he said, trying to calm the excited animal. "I'll never shoot this pistol straight if you don't stop pulling on the reins!"

Maybe they won't see me! Maybe they'll cross the clearing and ride into the path on the other side! Desperately he prayed that the men would do just that. Then he'd mount *Dusty*, go back to the road, and gallop away, leaving the men to chase him fruitlessly through the woods.

He heard the thundering of approaching hooves! First one, then the other of his pursuers burst from the trail and into his vision. The first rider, Ross, never looked at the cleared place in the forest. Andrew's heart leaped with hope.

But Sam glanced to both sides as his horse raced into the clearing—and saw Andrew at once! As Ross dashed across the burnt clearing and plunged out of sight in the woods beyond, Sam whipped his pistol around to his left and snapped a shot at Andrew.

But his galloping horse was going too fast for Sam to hit his target! Andrew aimed carefully as he tracked the rider from right to left, and fired. The big pistol bucked, and smoke and flame flashed from the barrel.

Andrew's bullet, too, though close, missed the moving target! Sam hauled his mount to a stop, and was pulling a long rifle from its scabbard as Andrew aimed again and squeezed the trigger. Again the big pistol bucked as flame and smoke burst from the second barrel.

With a cry, Sam tumbled from the saddle, striking the ground and rolling over. His horse bolted, dashing ahead after the first rider, and disappeared from sight. The wounded man groaned, and rolled on the ground in pain.

Andrew swung into the saddle and kicked *Dusty* into a rapid trot, heading back the way they had come. Thrusting his empty pistol into the holster, he gripped the reins with both hands and guided the stallion as best he could through the treacherous maze of branches that clutched at him from both sides. In a few moments he had reached the road. He swung *Dusty* onto this, turned the horse's head to his left, and kicked the stallion into a gallop.

The big horse leaped ahead, flying across the ground. Andrew wanted to pull the pistol out of the holster and reload, but he dared not release the reins. He bent low in the saddle, guiding the racing horse in a desperate race to the ferry.

After a while he slowed *Dusty* to a fast trot. Taking the pistol from its holster, he reached for his powder horn and bullet case and began to reload both barrels as he rode. Andrew had no way of knowing what that other rider, the first one through the clearing, was doing now; Andrew worried about this man.

Did he hear the shots? He must have! Did he figure out I'd come back to the road? he wondered. *Did he find his friend on the ground? If he did, would he stop and help him, or keep coming after me by himself?*

Andrew knew that he had to plan as if the remaining rider were still pursuing him. He also knew that when he reached the ferry, he could take cover, and pull out his long rifle. *I can deal with one rifleman, he thought grimly. Even if he's firing at me from the bank when the ferry leaves shore.*

Back in the woods, Ross had heard the shots from Sam's and Andrew's pistols. Startled, he hauled his horse to a stop, turned, and raced back toward the clearing. Suddenly Sam's horse crashed through the trees ahead and collided with his own. Ross was thrown from the saddle while the two frightened horses struck at each other with their hooves.

Sam's horse backed off, turned with difficulty in the narrow passage, and crashed back through the trees toward the clearing.

Ross, swearing mightily, scrambled to his feet—and was promptly knocked down by his wildly thrashing horse! Crawling desperately away from the animal's flailing hooves, Ross came to his feet again. Blood streamed from a deep cut on his cheek, and he fought to control his fury.

I'd better not scare that dumb animal away! he told himself. He dared not be left afoot in the woods. Calming himself, he tried to speak soothingly to the horse, trying to coax him to stay still so that he could grab the reins. Frantically he wondered what had happened back in the clearing.

Did they shoot each other? he wondered. *If they did, then I'll get Sam's share of the reward as well as my own!*

The horse backed away, almost panicking. Ross halted, bringing his mind back to the task at hand. He spoke softly again, pleadingly. Slowly the animal grew quiet. After a while—an eternity, it seemed to Ross!—he was able to walk up to the mount and seize the reins. Slowly, carefully, he eased himself into the saddle. Now he gave vent to his wrath. *What happened in the clearing?*

Riding with his pistol ready, he came into the clearing and pulled to a hasty halt as he saw his comrade lying on the ground. Glancing around quickly, he saw no sign of Andrew.

The boy got away! he realized, raging in his heart. Slowly he rode toward the fallen man, who was groaning with pain. The sight of his wounded partner enraged him. *That does it! I can't leave Sam here to be captured! The snake would tell everything he knew! I've got to get him back.*

Then the full reality hit him. *We've failed!*

Back on the road leading toward the ferry, Andrew finished reloading both barrels of the pistol. He thrust the long-barreled weapon into the holster in front of his knee, and kicked *Dusty* once more into a run. Glancing behind, he saw that there was no sign of his pursuer—not in the two or three hundred yards of road between him and the last bend, at least. Beyond that curve, trees covered the road from his sight. The other rider could be coming fast, and Andrew wouldn't be able to see him until he came around the bend.

Andrew knew he couldn't relax. He rode with grim urgency, knowing that his life depended on getting away. *Those men meant to kill me!* he thought. *To kill me—and take these messages!*

As he pondered the situation, Andrew realized suddenly that more was at stake than he had at first supposed. *But how did they know to follow Captain Innes to Shield's Tavern? How did they know he was going to send letters to Colonel Woodward? They sure came straight to the booth right by ours!*

The longer Andrew thought about this, the more obvious it became that there were spies in the ranks of the Patriots.

*Someone **told** about those letters to Colonel Woodward! he realized. Someone the Patriots think they can trust!*

He knew suddenly that it was not only vital that he get these messages to Virginia's Second Regiment; it was also vital that he return safely to Williamsburg. He *had* to tell Captain Innes that spies in the Patriot ranks had known of his mission and had tried to intercept him! Those spies had to be found—and stopped!—before they could do more damage to the Patriot cause!

He rode on, conscious of danger before him and danger behind. He began to feel very alone.

CHAPTER TEN

The Battle at Great Bridge

At last Andrew came in sight of the ferry. He'd seen no sign of his pursuers since leaving the clearing where he'd shot Sam from the saddle. At the bank of the river, however, he found half a dozen militiamen boarding the boat, along with another mounted traveler. Fervently Andrew thanked God that he'd gotten away from the pursuing men; he rode *Dusty* onto the ferry, and paid for his ride with a coin from the purse Captain Innes had given him.

Pulling his long rifle from its scabbard, he checked the powder in the pan, then walked to the rear of the ferry and scanned the shore. There was no sign of pursuit. While the other men glanced at him curiously, he kept careful watch on the shore. Slowly, ever so slowly, the ferry moved across the river.

"Looking for someone?" a big militiaman asked curiously.

"Sure am," Andrew replied quietly. He didn't elaborate, and the man didn't pursue the matter.

The boat crept, Andrew thought, with agonizing slowness across the James River. He began to think that the trip would take forever. Anxiously he scanned the northern shore for signs of his pursuers—but no one came to the landing. Gradually, as the boat moved farther and farther away from the dock, Andrew began to realize that he had escaped.

He realized suddenly that he'd been gripping the rifle barrel harder than he needed to! Deliberately he relaxed. A breeze moved across the water, a cold breeze this November day, and he pulled his collar up over his ears.

When the ferry finally reached the southern side of the river and docked, Andrew swung quickly into the saddle and walked *Dusty* onto shore. Then he put the big stallion into a gallop.

He spent the night with the same family that had put him up on his other trips for Captain Innes. The next morning, he was up early, and after a full breakfast resumed his trip. Later that morning he found the pickets of the Second Virginia Regiment. Identifying himself, he was taken to Colonel Woodward, who stood conversing with a group of his officers. Andrew was awed to find himself in the midst of hundreds of armed men.

Quickly the Colonel unfolded the letters, and read them. His face beamed when he read of the near approach of militiamen from North Carolina. But he was shocked to learn of the increasing size of Dunmore's forces.

"Dunmore beat one of our units the other day," the Colonel said with disgust, looking gravely at Andrew. "Never should have happened. Our men were set in an ambush at Kemp's Landing, waiting for the British and the Tories. But the nervous militiamen fired too soon—before Dunmore's men were in range—they gave themselves away, then scattered!"

Woodward shook his head at the foolish defeat. "We didn't lose so many men, twenty maybe, but the bad thing is that lots of people made up their minds that the Virginia militia couldn't beat Governor Dunmore! So they joined him! Now he's proclaimed that the whole Virginia Colony is in rebellion, and he's called for servants and slaves to join him and receive weapons to use against us!"

The Colonel looked somberly at Andrew. "Dunmore's no fool. He's a formidable opponent. And he knows how to hurt Virginia. He's captured some of our ships, and he's burnt some of our farms. He means to burn some towns, too, just like the British have done up north. If the government in London gives him the kind of military and naval support he's asked for, Virginia will be in terrible danger."

A tall militia officer standing beside the Colonel spoke up then.

"That's why we've got to beat him first, Colonel. Our scouts say he's fortified Great Bridge. He's built a small fort on a causeway between the swamp, he's got some soldiers and his own militia there, and he's gone back to Norfolk for more."

"Then we can't wait any longer!" Colonel Woodward said. "We've got to drive his men out of that fort before he can make it impregnable. We'll have to attack at once!"

Andrew learned later that Governor Dunmore's offer to free slaves did not apply to the Governor's own slaves, some fifty-seven persons in all. It only applied to the slaves of the Patriots.

But now the Colonel was gathering his officers. Andrew suddenly felt a hand on his shoulder, and heard a familiar voice:

"Boy, that's a mighty long gun you're carryin'. Know how to use it?"

"Matthew!" Andrew said, glad to see his old friend again. Matthew Anderson was the man who had taught him and Nathan how to fight in the woods, Indian-style; how to use knives and tomahawks; and how to reload their rifles while they ran. The woodsman gripped the boys hand and his weathered face broke into a broad grin. "Saw you come in the camp. Figured you'd want to finish your business with the Colonel. What brings you here?"

Swiftly Andrew told his friend of the messages Captain Innes had given him to bring to Colonel Woodward. "Militia units from North Carolina are on their way to help us!" he concluded excitedly.

The woodsman's face broke into a big grin. "I'm mighty glad to hear that!" Matthew said. "We could sure use their help, 'cause the Governor's had great success persuadin' some Virginia companies to switch sides and fight for the King! Especially in Norfolk, and Portsmouth, and along the coast, where the people can be hit by the British Navy. They're scared to death of being burned to the ground by the King's forces, and they've been cowed by Dunmore's successes so far. We can use help from North Carolina!"

Then the woodsman looked keenly at the boy. "Et anything recently?"

Andrew realized suddenly that he was starving. "Nope!" he replied. "Not for hours. Got any food?"

"We might find somethin'," Matthew said with a grin. "C'mon. I'll introduce you to the other scouts."

But Colonel Woodward called suddenly, "Matthew!"

Matthew turned instantly and walked over to the group of officers, Andrew at his heels.

"Matthew, we've got to move fast! Governor Dunmore's gone back to Norfolk to gather reinforcements for his fort at Great Bridge. He knows that if we can cross the river there, we'll intercept his food supplies from Norfolk and Princess Anne Counties. We've decided to take that fort before he can put more men it. We need your help."

"Certainly, Colonel," Matthew Anderson said gravely. "What can I do?"

"You're the one who scouted that fort for us when the Tories first built it," Colonel Woodward said. "You told us there's no way around it without going way 'round the swamp on either side."

"That's right," Matthew said. "It sits square by the road on the Elizabeth River. In the middle of the marshes. You can't get by easily—not if you want to stay dry, and keep your powder dry! Dunmore's picked the right place to stop our approach."

"Then we've got no choice," Colonel Woodward said. "We'll have to take that fort. We've decided to move against it first with snipers. I'd like you to lead some of our best shots to good positions. They'll start firin' at Dunmore's men during the day, and whittle down their numbers. We'll teach 'em to keep their heads down—while we get closer."

Another officer spoke up. "Pick a spot for us to put up some barricades, Matthew. We want to fire at 'em from the south, and from the east, if we can—catch 'em in a crossfire if they attack us."

"All right," Matthew said, "I'll do it." He turned to Andrew. "Want to help?"

"Yes, sir," Andrew replied.

"Get your horse," Matthew said. "We'll ride as close as we can. But first," he said with a wink to Andrew, "I'll get you somethin' to eat!"

An hour later, Matthew, Andrew, and a score of men in hunting shirts, all carrying their deadly long rifles, crept through a patch of woods to the south of the small British fort. Matthew stopped the riflemen at the edge of the woods, right beside a small wooden church that sat in a fork in the road. Before them stretched a row of houses, lining the road on both sides.

"There's the fort," he pointed. "Right past that little island."

"There's a bridge 'cross the water," one of the men remarked, as he rechecked the powder in the pan of his rifle.

"Yep, there is," Matthew replied. "Or, there was. The British tore up some of the planks so we couldn't get at 'em. You men stay here a while. Aim at the windows of those near houses, 'case someone takes a notion to shoot at me. I'm going to scout those other woods."

The woodsman flattened himself on the ground, long rifle cradled in his arms, and began to crawl from the woods toward the small church. He crawled past this, and went on into the woods on the other side. Then he was lost to sight.

He was back within half an hour. "I've found where we can make a barricade," he said. "We'll have 'em in a crossfire if they try to drive us away."

Swiftly he explained the terrain. Then he told one of the men to ride back to the regiment. "Tell the Colonel to send some more men," Matthew said. "And tell him to send us axemen. We'll make some barricades, and our riflemen firin' from those will make those British keep their heads down.

The man went to his horse, swung into the saddle, and galloped back to the regiment.

"Sure there's no people in those houses?" one of the men asked.

"They fled when the British built that fort," Matthew said. "But just to be sure, let's look."

Several men volunteered for the task. They spread out and approached the houses that lined the road. One by one, they searched these. Then the men reached the bank of the narrow river. Here one of them turned back, and waved.

"It's clear," Matthew said. "Here's what we'll do." Swiftly he explained his plan. Then he led half the men toward the west, through the woods, to a piece of rising ground that was in rifle range of the small British fort.

Meanwhile, Andrew and the other riflemen formed a skirmish line and began to move past the empty houses toward the edge of the marsh. It was cold, but Andrew found himself sweating as he walked slowly through the thick grass toward the causeway that led to the island. The men went through this and found themselves nearing the bank. Here the ground became suddenly lower, and their way was blocked by the marsh and its water.

"There's a sentry!" one of the riflemen said suddenly.

They all could see the red-coated soldier standing on the causeway nearest to the island that led to the fort.

"I'll drop him," someone said.

The rifleman rose to his feet, took careful aim, and fired.

The sentry fell, dropping his long musket. Cries of rage rose from a group of men the Virginians couldn't see. Puffs of smoke, followed by the sound of firing, burst from a clump of bushes on the near side of the small island.

"Too far," one man spat contemptuously. "They've just got muskets."

The riflemen spread out along the bank of the marsh, and began to fire as they saw targets. Some of the Britishers and Tories fired back. And some had rifles, for bullets began to whistle close!

"Take care, Boys," a man called. "They've got riflemen!"

The men heeded the warning and dropped to the ground. Crawling forward, they sought good positions, and began to fire from behind small rises in the ground. But when the light began to fade with the setting sun, the men withdrew and returned to camp. Colonel Woodward replaced them with other scouts to watch the British during the night, and warn of any surprise attack.

For over a week the riflemen would fire at Dunmore's troops during the day, then pull back at dark. Southeast of the fort, the Patriots built two barricades on a mound that rose from the marsh. From this position they could keep up a continuous fire on the British and their Tory allies.

"When's the Colonel going to attack?" Andrew asked Matthew one morning, as they moved toward their position behind the barricade. He was anxious to return to Williamsburg and warn Capt. Innes of the spies who'd known of his mission—but he hadn't had the heart to leave Matthew and the other men.

"He's waiting for powder and shot," Matthew replied. "We don't have much. He's sent messengers back begging for more supplies."

"I think most of the men would rather have blankets," Andrew said. "They're freezing at night."

"I know they are. Thank the Lord you and I brought ours. I just can't figure why the Committee in Williamsburg won't send the Colonel what he asks for! They want us to attack—but the Colonel's asking for a couple of small cannons to deal with the cannons the British have got in their fort."

"Why doesn't he order a charge?" Andrew asked.

"See that narrow causeway, Boy?" Matthew asked. "It's so narrow that only five or six men can walk side by side. If the British used grape shot in their cannons, our men would be slaughtered before they crossed the bridge and the causeway. The Colonel wants some cannon to knock down that fort, and sweep the causeway with our own grapeshot, before he sends his men across."

"But some of the younger officers are pushing him to do something," Andrew said. "I heard 'em talking last night. They think we should move against the fort before the Governor brings reinforcements to strengthen it."

"Well, I think so, too," Matthew Anderson agreed somberly. "Personally, I think we can wipe out their cannoneers with our riflemen, and get close enough to charge 'em."

A few days later a group of North Carolina militiamen joined the Virginia Second Regiment. This cheered the Virginians immensely. They'd been on short rations ever since a Loyalist had blown up Bachelor Mill Dam, thus destroying the bridge over Deep Creek. This was the shortest way to Suffolk and its supplies, and was a damaging blow to the Patriots. So the arrival of the North Carolinians with more supplies gave the Virginians a lift.

"But they didn't bring any cannon!" Matthew Anderson said bitterly. "And that's what the Colonel's waiting for."

The sniping by day grew more intense. And downstream, Patriots and Loyalists fought each other several times. Each group gathered boats with which to attack the other by surprise. But premature firing gave away the Patriot's attack, and they had to withdraw. They tried again—but were spotted by Loyalists in wagons from Norfolk, and had to turn back.

But the Second Regiment was blocking Norfolk's food supplies from Princess Anne and Norfolk Counties, and the seaport city was feeling the pinch. And Governor Dunmore— former Governor, now—was growing impatient. When a runaway slave told him that there were only a couple of hundred Virginians around the fort at Great Bridge, Dunmore decided to attack and break the stalemate.

Dunmore also heard troubling news: a large body of North Carolina militia *with cannons* was just a day's march away! Once the Patriots put cannons in place, they could knock down his small wooden fort, cross the river, and march on Norfolk before he'd finished the fortifications he was building to defend the town.

Dunmore called for a meeting of the British and Tory officers to make plans to attack the American forces that were besieging the fort at Great Bridge.

But the officers of the British 14th Regiment were appalled when Dunmore told them he wanted their men to charge the Patriots' position across the causeway. The English soldiers had been sent originally to provide protection for the former Governor, not make frontal attacks on rebel positions in the interests of Norfolk merchants! But Dunmore had drawn them deeper and deeper into his military schemes, and the officers felt that now was the time to draw back.

They urged him not to throw away the lives of their soldiers by a frontal attack on the Second Virginia Regiment.

But the Governor was the senior British officer in Virginia, and he was in complete command. Firmly he overrode the army officers' objections and ordered Captain Leslie to make plans to cross the causeway and the bridge.

"I want that so-called 'Regiment' destroyed, Captain!" Dunmore said, his face red with anger at the continued frustration the Patriots had caused to his plans. "Scatter them into the marsh, hunt them down man by man, destroy the lot of 'em! With Norfolk as our base, the King's forces can divide Virginia in two and knock her out of this mad rebellion!"

Captain Leslie had no course but to obey. He'd brought a force of sixty Loyalists, one hundred and twenty British soldiers, and some armed sailors from the fleet. And Dunmore had already put a hundred of his men in the fort.

"These will be quite sufficient," the Governor had said confidently. "Those militiamen can't stand against British Regulars. They'll scatter like chaff in the wind!"

The British force left Norfolk and marched hard, arriving at the fort early in the morning of December 9. They'd marched for twelve hours, and were dead-tired; Captain Leslie decided to let them rest.

Across the causeway from the fort, the Virginia militiamen of the Second Regiment had had no warning of the British reinforcements. That night they shivered in their scant blankets through the hours of darkness, expecting to wake up to another frustrating day of long-range sniping.

Andrew and Matthew had put some barrels around one side of a supply wagon to break the wind, arranged their blankets beside the barrels, and were fairly comfortable in the cold nights—more so than a lot of the men. But they all were tired of the siege, of the short rations, and of their cold camp.

"How long will the Colonel wait, Matthew?" Andrew asked in the dark, as he waited for sleep. "Governor Dunmore's going to bring more men sometime—the Colonel can't wait forever!"

"You're right, Boy," Matthew replied. "He can't."

The morning drums brought the men of the Second Regiment awake. They rose, ate, gathered their gear, and went about their usual daily routine.

Captain Leslie had chosen not to attack before the Patriot's morning drums awoke the colonial militia. Contemptuous of the rebel's capacity to stand against a bayonet charge of his redcoats, he'd waited until the Virginians were awake and moving about their camp. Then he sent his men to lay down the planks they'd taken from the bridge, and swiftly threw his men across the river to the small island.

The Patriots' scouts fired a few shots at the advancing British, and retreated to the mainland, leaving Captain Leslie in control of the island. Leslie brought up his cannon, then ordered Lieutenant Fordyce to lead an infantry charge across the causeway.

"Rush that barricade!" he commanded. "Then charge with the bayonet! The rebels will melt away like the winter snow!"

The Patriots had become so used to periodic firing by both their own and the British pickets, that at first they were not alarmed by the shooting. But when it continued, then intensified, Captain Travis, who commanded the colonials' advance guard, realized that the British were indeed taking the offensive! Calling his men to the barricade, he told them to hold their fire until the English were at point blank range. His eighty men waited nervously behind their wooden shelter, rifles aimed at the white belts that crossed the red-coated chests of the charging British soldiers.

Andrew and Matthew ran to their posts at the barricades to the east of the causeway, where a company of militiamen from Culpeper under Colonel Stevens was waiting for the British to attack. They quickly joined a file of men behind the logs, and aimed their long rifles at the charging British. Andrew's heart was pounding and his rifle wavered. Grimly he got control of himself, took several deep breaths, then steadied his long weapon again on the white belts that crossed the red coat of an advancing British soldier. The cold wooden stock of the rifle numbed his cheek as he waited for the command to fire.

"The fools!" Matthew said softly. "Why are they throwing away the advantage of their position? We've got 'em in a crossfire!"

It was true. The Virginia militiamen faced the charging British from behind the barricade on the road, as well as from the barricades to the right flank of the redcoats where Matthew and Andrew and the Culpeper militia waited with aimed rifles.

Then they heard the shout from the Patriot's barricade at the end of the causeway: "Fire!"

A blast of smoke and flame and lead swept from the Patriot's rifles and crumpled the yelling British formation. Men fell in heaps, whole groups of them. Captain Fordyce was killed at once, and the British lieutenant was wounded. The attack suddenly faltered. The English fired back, but their ranks were collapsing. Then the shocked survivors retreated, firing as they did so. Running frantically back to the island, they shot sporadically at the pursuing Virginia militia.

"Fire" called Colonel Stevens. The rifles of the Culpeper militia burst into flame, and more British were hit from the flank. The redcoats and their allies fled into the wooden fort as the Second Regiment approached across the bridge and reached the causeway, firing continually as they advanced.

In thirty minutes it was over. A white flag waved above the ramparts of the fort, and the British called for a truce. Captain Fordyce and two other officers had been killed, fourteen soldiers were dead, and fifty more of their men wounded. The Second Regiment had one man slightly wounded.

The fort was taken. Colonel Woodward buried the brave Captain Fordyce with full military honors, and sent a message to Dunmore assuring him that the prisoners were receiving good care. The Loyalists and former slaves were tied together and marched to Williamsburg as prisoners of war.

Around noon, Colonel Woodward called Andrew to his tent. When he arrived, Andrew saw Matthew Anderson walk up with a group of the militia officers. The men were in great high spirits.

"Congratulations, Colonel," Matthew said with a broad grin. "You broke 'em!"

"Thank you, Matthew," the Colonel grinned in reply. "We did, indeed. This was not a big battle—but I think it will prove to be a decisive one. Governor Dunmore can't hold Norfolk if we keep his forces and the townspeople from getting food from the countryside. We'll march closer to the city, now, and block the roads. With the North Carolina men, we've got a strong enough force to bottle him up. I don't think he can maintain himself in Norfolk for long. This small battle may indeed prove to be as significant here in the South as was the battle of Bunker Hill in the North."

"Meantime," the Colonel said, turning to Andrew, and holding out a thick canvass envelope, "here's my report to the Committee in Williamsburg. Take this to them right away! Ride as fast as you can! They've got to know what we've done! Tell them I'll be moving the regiment closer to Norfolk as soon as we get our supplies. Tell them I think we've about got Dunmore bottled up!"

"Yes, sir," Andrew said, elated at the prospect of returning home. He turned and headed toward the tree where *Dusty* was tethered.

Matthew Anderson walked with Andrew to his horse. The woodsman's lean face was solemn as he gave the boy a final warning. "Stay alert on the way, Andrew. The countryside's swarming with the Governor's scouts and spies. Don't relax for a minute! Don't confide in anyone. You can't tell who's a Patriot or who's a Tory in this part of the country! And you can't always be sure in Williamsburg!"

Andrew nodded solemnly. He checked the powder in his big two-barreled pistol; then he checked his rifle. Both guns were ready.

Andrew was ready too, and anxious to get back to Williamsburg.

He shook hands with his friend, stepped into the saddle, and put *Dusty* into a fast trot.

Wonder if I'll run into the Governor's men on the way home? he thought. Andrew pulled the long rifle from its scabbard and rested it across the saddle in front of him.

CHAPTER ELEVEN

There She Is! And She's Alone!

Sarah emerged from the back door of the kitchen to find Wilbur waiting with her horse at the porch steps.

"Belle's saddled and waiting for you, Sarah," the big man said.

"Thank you, Wilbur," she smiled, walking down the steps and handing him the cloth-covered basket of food her mother had prepared.

Wilbur took this from her, set it on the ground, handed her the reins, then stooped and cupped his hands. Sarah placed her foot in his hands, and he lifted her to the side-saddle. Then he tied the basket behind her saddle.

He stepped back and grinned. "Don't let any of those militiamen talk you out of that food, Sarah! I can smell it—and they will too!"

"Don't worry," she laughed. "I'm not going near their camp, so I won't have any trouble. Thank you."

Wilbur glanced at the sky. "Won't be long before it starts to get dark. You hurry back."

"I will," she said. "I'm not going far."

She rode out of the yard, turned *Belle*, and trotted toward the street. Ordinarily, Rachel would have ridden with her. Mrs. Anthony was expecting the birth of her child any day now, and Sarah's and Rachel's mothers had been taking turns sending their two girls with a cooked meal to help out the expectant mother and her family. But, this day, Rachel was taking a basket to another family who was just recovering from flu. So Sarah rode alone.

Sarah enjoyed the sense of freedom as she rode by herself along the pleasant street. People on foot and on horse were hurrying home at the approach of darkness. A wagon piled high with empty barrels plodded along the way Sarah was going, and Sarah trotted *Belle* swiftly past.

Thank goodness there are no marching militiamen in the street! she thought to herself. Sometimes the militia drummers made horses nervous, and she shuddered at the thought of the basket of hot food being thrown to the ground by the violent reactions of a frightened mount!

She turned onto Francis Street and rode in the direction of the Powder Magazine. Finally Sarah pulled *Belle* to a stop before a one storey gray house. Dismounting, she tied *Belle's* reins to a post. Reaching up, she untied the basket from behind the saddle, patted *Belle*, then let herself through the gate and walked to the door.

Standing behind a thick tree trunk several houses down the street, Stephen Bancroft and John watched Sarah enter the house with the basket on her arm.

"That's her!" Stephen said. "That's the Edwards girl!"

"Your father's servant was right!" John said triumphantly. "He said that the girl was bringing food to that woman this week. But he said the other girl was with her. Today—she's alone!"

"She is indeed alone," Stephen said, his mouth twisting into a bitter smile. "I learned that the other girl is taking food from her mother to another family, and that she'll be doing this for a week at least! And this Edwards girl will be bringing food for Mrs. Anthony until the baby is born."

Stephen turned and grinned triumphantly as he explained his father's scheme to John. "Mr. Anthony's at the militia camp past the College, fixing wagons. He doesn't come back till after dark. Hurry! Run tell Father that the Edwards girl's alone at the Anthony's, and that this is a good time to capture her! She'll help Mrs. Anthony feed the younger kids, and will be here for another hour—she usually leaves just before it's dark. Ride back at once, and bring the wagon!"

"And then?" John asked, knowing the answer, and savoring the revenge they'd have by capturing this meddlesome girl.

"Then we'll wait for the girl to walk to her horse, grab her suddenly, throw her in the wagon and tie her up! We'll take her to the Governor right away! Then he'll get some answers! He'll find out how the Rebels are using these young people as spies!"

John untied his horse, leaped into the saddle, and kicked his mount into a gallop. Stephen lounged casually against the tree, where he could keep an eye on the house. He was gloating.

At last we'll get that girl! She and her friends have interfered too often in the Governor's plans to be innocent—they're Patriot spies! And the Governor will hold her hostage until her father surrenders. Then he'll be hung for the traitor he is!

At the Anthony house, Lindsey opened the door at Sarah's knock, and beamed with delight when she saw her friend. "Come in! Oh, thank you so much, Sarah!"

Lindsey was a lovely girl of twelve, and with her younger sisters, Mary, and Laurie, was quite capable of caring for the two small boys and managing their home during the last stages of their mother's pregnancy. But the Edwards and the Hendricks had always been close to this family, and insisted on helping the Anthony's by bringing a basket of food each afternoon.

Mary and Laurie rushed up as Sarah entered, and gave their friend a hug. Mary took the basket to the kitchen and began to set out the food while the other girls went into the bedroom to visit with Mrs. Anthony.

"Sarah, you're an angel—again!" Mrs. Anthony said with a grateful smile. A cheerful woman, she hadn't been feeling well the past several days, and had had to rest more than usual. She was propped up in her bed, reading.

"Mother sends her greetings, Mrs. Anthony," Sarah said. "We're all praying for you each day. How do you feel?"

"Tired," Mrs. Anthony laughed, "but that's to be expected. I always get real tired around this time. It won't be long now!"

"Where's Rachel?" Mary asked. A pretty dark haired girl, Mary was the same age as Rachel, and the two were close friends.

"She's taking some food to the Harrison's," Sarah said, sitting down in the chair by the bed. "They've had the flu!"

"She'd better not catch that!" Mrs. Anthony said.

"No, Ma'am," Sarah replied. "She won't go in. But she's sorry she couldn't come here. She'll be back with me next week, she thinks."

While Sarah visited with the Anthonys, John was returning with Mr. Bancroft's servant in a wagon. He rode on the wagon-seat beside the servant, who drove the horses as quickly as he could without attracting undue attention to their passage through the town. They crossed the Duke of Gloucester Street, turned, and hurried toward Queen Street. John's face was flushed with excitement.

"We'll finally capture that girl!" he gloated aloud.

"How'll you get her to the Governor, Sir?" the big man beside him asked.

"We'll wait by the house until she comes out. Then, as she starts to get on her horse, we'll grab her, gag her, wrap her in the blanket, and put her in the back of the wagon. Stephen will help. Then we'll head toward Bruton Parish Church."

"But if there's any pursuit, we can't escape in a slow wagon!"

"Don't worry. There'll be a carriage waiting beside the church, just around the corner and across from the Palace Green. We'll transfer the girl to the carriage, you'll drive the empty wagon back to the shop, and the carriage will take her to a plantation on the river. There's a boat that docks there all the time. The owner pretends he's a Patriot, but he's really loyal to the Crown. He takes messages to and from the Governor in Norfolk."

"I thought that the Patriots discovered that boat," the man replied.

"They discovered one boat, all right," John snarled. "All because of that girl and her friend! But we've got others. We've got more spies than the Patriots realize, in fact. But it is dangerous. That's why we've got to get the girl out of this slow wagon and into a fast carriage. Also, should anyone connect a wagon with her kidnaping, they'll not suspect a carriage. And if anyone stops you in the road in their search for her, your wagon will be empty."

"Won't the family she's visiting see us capture her?" the man asked. He didn't like anything about this.

"Won't matter," John said with a smirk. "The father works till after dark each night, the mother's in bed, and there's just some young girls at home with her. By the time those girls can get help, you'll be riding an empty wagon to the shop, the carriage will have taken the girl out of town, and no one will have any idea where to look for her!"

But John became frustrated by the slow pace of the wagon. "Can't you make these horses go any faster?" he complained. "This is taking longer than I'd figured!"

"But Mr. Bancroft said we weren't to attract any attention," the servant replied defensively. "He said he'd be ruined if anyone connected his wagon with a kidnaping."

"I know, I know!" John snapped. Slowly the wagon moved along the street, the clop-clop-clopping of the horses' hooves sounding louder and louder in John's ears.

Andrew had returned to Williamsburg just half an hour before. He'd taken the message from Colonel Woodward to Captain Innes, told of the battle, and of the Colonel's plans, and had received the captain's warm thanks. Then he'd told of the possibility of spies in the Patriots' ranks.

"Someone knew that you'd given me those messages!" he told the captain.

Shocked, Captain Innes told Andrew he'd look into this right away. He thanked the boy warmly.

Now, Andrew was on his way home. He rode wearily past his own house and dismounted at the Edwards' back porch. *I'll stop at her place first*, he thought. He hoped Sarah would be able to come with him while he took care of the stallion. *But I'll have to tell her I wasn't in any danger!* he reminded himself as he climbed the steps and approached the back door.

There was a cheery glow from the windows beside the door, and as he knocked Andrew felt the strain and care of the past weeks begin to slip away, like a cloak falling from his shoulders. The door was opened, and Mrs. Edwards greeted him with great delight, hugging him warmly. "Andrew, I'm so glad you're back! Seems like you've been gone a lifetime!"

"Yes, Ma'am," he replied with a grin. "Seems like that to me, too! Actually, I haven't even gone home yet. I was wondering if Sarah could visit with me while I took care of the stallion? I'll walk her back to the house when I finish."

"I know she would want to, Andrew, but she's taken a basket of food to the Anthonys'."

Mrs. Edwards glanced up at the sky, and frowned. "It's getting dark already," she noted, "and in fact I'm a little surprised that she hasn't returned. Would you mind riding over and escorting her back? She got a late start this afternoon—it was my fault—but I did want her back while there's still some light. I'd feel better knowing she wasn't riding back home alone."

"Yes, Ma'am!" Andrew said quickly. "I know where the Anthonys' live. I'll ride back with her!"

"Thank you, Andrew!" she said gratefully. "You'll most likely meet her on the way."

Andrew's weariness was gone now at the thought of riding home with Sarah. Walking quickly off the porch, he stepped into the saddle and trotted the stallion out of the yard. Once into the street, he kicked his heels lightly against *Dusty's* ribs, and the powerful horse broke into a gallop.

"How can he still want to gallop after a day on the road?" Andrew thought with a grin. *Seems like he's got new strength just by coming home! So have I!* His own spirits had lifted also. He'd get to ride back with Sarah, and she'd talk with him while he unsaddled and brushed down the stallion!

Several blocks away, Mr. Bancroft's wagon turned again, and headed for the Anthonys' house.

"She's still there!" John said with relief, as he saw *Belle* standing tied to the rail.

"There's Mr. Stephen," the servant said. The tall blond man had just stepped out from behind the tree, and was walking toward them.

"Pull the wagon closer," Stephen said quickly as he approached. "We'll wait for her to come out to her horse before we grab her."

"What if the family sees us capture her?" the servant asked Stephen. He was very nervous about this assignment. He knew the laws against kidnaping.

"If those Anthony girls stay at the door while Sarah goes to her horse, then you walk up and talk to 'em," Stephen replied. "Ask when their father will return."

"That's a good idea, Stephen!" John said.

Stephen smiled. "That'll distract 'em, you see." He turned back to the servant. "And if you block the door while you're talking with 'em, they won't be able to see past you. John and I will come behind Sarah and grab her when she starts to mount. We'll cover her mouth so she can't yell, and lift her in the wagon and wrap a gag around her and tie her hands and feet. We'll throw a blanket over her, and hold her there while you come back and start the horses going. Even if those girls are still standing in the doorway, they won't notice a thing!"

Eagerly the three men moved closer to the house and waited for Sarah to end her visit with the Anthony's. Stephen and John stood behind the thick trunk of one tree, while John leaned against another. A horseman galloped past and the three stiffened in alarm. But the rider kept going, and the watchers relaxed.

"It's getting dark!" John observed. "She's got to be coming soon!"

"The later she comes, the better it is for us!" Stephen replied. "We can use all the dark we can get!"

"Yes, but you know her folks won't let her wait till dark."

Suddenly the door of the house opened, and a girl stepped out.

"Hush!" Stephen said quietly. "She's coming!"

Sarah stood on the porch for a moment, speaking with Lindsey. Then she gave her friend a quick hug, and walked toward *Belle*.

Lindsey held the door open, watching her.

John cursed. "That Anthony girl is still watching her!"

Stephen was about to order the servant to go to the door and distract Lindsey, when one of her sisters called her from within the house.

"Coming!" Lindsey replied. "Bye, Sarah," she called, her lovely green eyes shining with gratitude. "Thank you so much!"

"You're welcome, Lindsey," Sarah said, as she untied *Belle*. "See you tomorrow."

It was perfectly timed. As Lindsey closed the door of her house, Stephen and John stepped quickly from behind the tree, came up behind Sarah, and swiftly grabbed her. She was busy putting her foot in the stirrup, and never saw them approach. Before she could cry out, Stephen's big hand was over her mouth and his arm around her waist. She felt herself being lifted, then thrown roughly into a wagon. A gag was wrapped quickly around her mouth—but not before she had bit deeply into the big hand that had kept her silent.

Cursing with the sudden pain, Stephen tied the cloth around the girl's mouth as John tied her hands behind her back. Throwing a blanket over her, John and Stephen sat beside her and then bound her feet as well. The servant climbed onto the wagon seat, took up the reins, and released the long handle of the brake. Flipping the reins on the backs of the horses, he set the wagon in motion.

But Lindsey had returned suddenly to the front door of her house. "Sarah!" she called out, "you forgot your book!"

Lindsey was surprised to see *Belle* still tied to the rail, without any sign of Sarah. Then she observed the wagon moving away. Rushing out of the house toward *Belle*, she saw one man on the wagon seat, and the heads of two others sitting behind him in the wagon. The men paid no attention to her as she called again, "Sarah!" Lindsey looked frantically around for signs of the missing girl.

But Sarah was nowhere to be seen.

Lindsey called out again: "Sarah!"

Then she ran back into the house and called for Mary. Rushing into her mother's room, Lindsey told the startled woman that Sarah had disappeared. "There's a wagon with three men in it riding away!" she said in wild alarm. "It was right in front of the house, and now its going away! There are two men in the back, just sitting there, and I know they've got Sarah!"

Mary rushed to her side. "But why would anyone capture Sarah?" she cried, her dark eyes wide with shock.

"I don't know—but she's got to be in that wagon!" Lindsey replied. "That's the only place she could be—her horse is still here and she's not in the street! I looked all around! She just disappeared in a moment!" She leaped up and turned toward the door. "I'll look for help, Mother!" Lindsey said, rushing from the room. Mary was at her heels.

The two burst out of the front door and ran to the street. Their anguished eyes saw the wagon with its men moving swiftly away.

"Can you catch that wagon?" Mary asked, her mind racing.

"Maybe I can—if I ride *Belle*," Lindsey replied. "But I couldn't make those men stop."

Then she thought aloud. "But I could follow them! And you could follow me! And Laurie could follow you! And if we keep each other in sight, one of us surely will see *someone* who can help us! And we can call them and tell them what's happening! Quick! Tell Mother! Tell her we'll stay away from those men, but that we'll just keep them in sight until we can find some men!"

"I'll get Laurie, too!" Mary said, running back into the house.

Lindsey walked carefully up to Sarah's horse and began to talk softly. She'd ridden *Belle* before, and the animal knew her well. Slowly she gathered the reins in her hands, then put her foot in the stirrup and pulled herself up into the side-saddle. She wasn't used to doing this without help, but she managed, and settled herself in the saddle.

Belle stepped nervously into the street, but Lindsey kept a firm grip on the reins, and turned the horse after the wagon.

Mary and Laurie rushed out of the house into the falling dusk.

"Mother says to be careful, Lindsey!" Mary called. "Don't get close to the wagon!"

"I won't," Lindsey called back. "And you two stay in the distance! But keep in sight of each other! I know we'll find some men to rescue Sarah!"

She trotted *Belle* after the wagon, which had already reached the corner. "It's turning toward Duke of Gloucester Street!" she called back to Mary.

Mary, forty yards behind Lindsey and *Belle*, passed this news to little Laurie, who was walking some distance behind her.

Thus the strange cavalcade of three young girls, one mounted, two hurrying on foot, proceeded to the corner, in the trail of the wagon which was now far ahead.

In the wagon, the men had heard the girls' voices calling for their friend. Looking back, they could see the dim form of *Belle* coming after them.

"I heard those girls calling 'Sarah' when we pulled away!" John said to Stephen, his face anxious. "And I think one of those girls in on the horse? See there?"

"I do," Stephen replied. "But it won't do 'em any good. They can't see Sarah in the wagon. And that girl on the horse sure can't stop us!" He laughed. "This worked perfectly! Now the Governor'll make this girl and her family pay for being spies for the rebels! Don't look back any more! Just pretend we have nothing to worry about."

Lindsey's and Mary's and Laurie's hopes that they'd spot men in the street whom they could call for help began to dim. For some reason, there was no one else in sight!

I should have run to the house next door! Lindsey thought to herself. *But I know Mr. Morgan's not home yet!*

Now, the three girls began to doubt whether or not they'd be able to find men to rescue Sarah. There was just no one in sight.

The strange little cavalcade moved through the street in the gathering darkness. The wagon led; some sixty yards behind rode Lindsey on *Belle*; Mary now hurried about the same distance behind Lindsey, and behind her, little Laurie struggled to keep up.

Oh, please, Lord, Lindsey prayed silently, *Please send someone to help us!*

Chapter Twelve

Show what You Can Do with Your Fists!

Andrew galloped *Dusty* through the falling darkness, thankful that the streets were empty. But as he noticed the coming of evening, his joy at the thought of riding home with Sarah gave way to a strange foreboding.

She should be on her way home by now! he thought. I should have met her already. He was surprised to find almost no one on the street. *They're all inside their homes*, he guessed.

He galloped on and came close to the Anthony's block when suddenly he saw a young girl standing in the intersection of a crossing street. Startled, he pulled *Dusty* to a prancing stop. He was surprised to recognize Laurie Anthony.

"Laurie!" he called, "what are you doing in the street? It's getting dark!"

"Oh, Andrew," she cried, running up to him, "Sarah's been captured. They're taking her away in a wagon! Lindsey and Mary and I are following them! Oh, I'm so glad to see you!"

"Sarah captured?" Andrew replied, stunned. "What do you mean?"

"Sarah brought Mother a basket of food. Then she left to go home. But she forgot her book. And when Lindsey ran out the door to give it to her, Sarah had disappeared! *Belle* was still standing at the rail, but Sarah wasn't on her. And a wagon with three men in it was just going away!"

"Three men in a wagon?" Andrew asked sharply.

"Yes! We know those men took Sarah in that wagon! Mary's down the street, and Lindsey's ahead of Mary, riding *Belle*. She's following the wagon! We're all following each other, and we're hoping we'll find some men to rescue her! Thank Heavens you came!"

"Goodness you're brave, Laurie! But wait here for Mary! Don't go any farther! I'll send Mary back and you two go home and tell the neighbors. Lindsey and I will follow that wagon and get help!"

Andrew turned *Dusty* and kicked him into a gallop, racing down the street to Mary.

He pulled the excited stallion to a stop, and called out, "Mary! Go back with Laurie!" he called. "Call the neighbors and tell them what happened! I'll send Lindsey back as soon as I see where that wagon's going!"

"Oh, Andrew, thank God you've come!" Mary said, turning and running back to her younger sister.

Andrew marveled at the courage of these young girls to persist in following Sarah's kidnappers. *What a family!* he thought.

In the gathering darkness Andrew could make out Lindsey farther ahead on *Belle*. He slowed *Dusty* to a trot, suddenly realizing that he just couldn't rush headlong at the wagon without a plan. He couldn't afford to alert those men that they were being followed—not until he knew what he was going to do. Slowly he caught up with *Belle*.

He rode up behind her and called her name: "Lindsey!"

"Andrew!" she said, and burst into tears.

"Oh, Andrew, Sarah's in that wagon! She'd left our house, and was about to ride home, but she left her book in mother's room. When I saw it, I went to the door to call her back. But she wasn't in sight! *Belle* was standing there, but Sarah was gone! And that wagon was going away, with three men in it. I *know* those men captured her and hid her in the wagon!"

"I know. Mary told me. You girls are wonderfully brave to follow like you did!" Andrew said. "But we've got to think how to rescue her."

"We just knew we'd find some men to call and help us," Lindsey said. "But the street's deserted! There's no one! Until you came!"

"I told Mary to go back with Laurie," Andrew said, his brain racing. "If you can stay with me a little longer, I'd be grateful. I told Mary I'd send you back when I learned where they were taking Sarah. Your sisters will have roused the neighbors by then, and you can send help."

"Oh, I *will*" she said. "I'll do anything to help you rescue Sarah!"

"Let's get out of the street, and ride over in front of the houses, behind the line of trees, Lindsey!" Andrew said suddenly. "That way, they won't see us so easily. I think the trees will help hide us."

Andrew pulled *Dusty* to the right, then trotted him between the trees and the houses. Lindsey did the same, trotting Belle just beside *Dusty*.

In the wagon ahead, Stephen sneaked a glance behind. "That horse has gone!" he said to his companions. "I told you we had nothing to fear from that young girl!"

But the horse was *not* gone. Stephen just didn't see it behind the row of trees on the side of the road. Had he looked more carefully he would have spotted not one but two horses following them!

Suddenly Lindsey noticed that the wagon had reached Duke of Gloucester Street, and had changed course.

"The wagon's turning, Andrew!" Lindsey said.

Peering between a gap in the trees, Andrew saw that she was right; the wagon was turning to their left.

"They're heading toward the College!" he said, a puzzled frown on his face. "Why are they staying in the middle of town like this? If they've kidnaped somebody I'd think they'd ride out of town right away—not go down the main street!"

"But they didn't seem too worried about me following them. They aren't worried about being chased!"

"I don't think they realized that you'd kept on their trail," Andrew replied. "And maybe they didn't see me join you. But they had to know someone *might* see 'em capture her! They've got to have a plan!"

"Maybe they're going to keep her in town," Lindsey suggested.

Lanterns on their posts threw patches of light on the darkening street. And from both sides candles and lanterns in the houses shed their faint light into the falling darkness. Andrew realized suddenly that Mrs. Anthony would be frightened at the absence of her oldest girl. Mary and Laurie should be home by now, he thought, but she'd sure be worrying about Lindsey.

"Lindsey, I should send you home so your mother won't fret!" he said bleakly.

"But then you won't have any one to send a message back when you see where they're taking Sarah!" she replied. "Andrew, I won't leave you as long as Sarah needs us!"

He leaned from the saddle and patted her shoulder. "Lindsey, I knew you were kind, 'cause everyone knows that. But now I know how brave you are! But you're shivering! I didn't realize you didn't have your coat!"

Quickly he pulled off his long coat and threw it around her shoulders. The grateful girl wrapped the coat around her and thanked him.

They followed the wagon down the wide street. For some reason, there was no sign of other horsemen or wagons. The street was empty—except for the wagon ahead. Andrew wondered if he could send Lindsey to one of the houses they passed. *But if the folks don't know her, they might not believe her message!* he realized. *And then when I see where the wagon's taking Sarah, I wouldn't have anyone to send for help; I've got to keep Lindsey with me till I know where they're going!*

But as they approached Greenhow's store, Andrew saw the building ablaze with light. *There'll be men here who can help us! he thought.*

"Lindsey, there's lights in Mr. Greenhow's store! My family knows them! Yours does too! Ride to the door and knock. Tell them what happened, and ask then to send some men after me at once! Tell them I'm following those kidnappers toward the College! I'll ride closer to the wagon!"

"But Andrew, you can't attack three men by yourself!"

"I've got a pistol," he said grimly. "I'll make 'em stop until you send help! Hurry, now. And thank you!"

"Be careful, Andrew!" she said, as she wheeled *Belle* and trotted her toward Greenhow's Store. Leaping to the ground from the side-saddle, the reins gripped firmly in her hands, she led *Belle* to the rail and swiftly tied her. Then she ran to the door and pounded the knocker with all her might. Glancing across the street, she could no longer see Andrew and *Dusty*. Nor could she see the wagon.

Oh, I hope someone comes! she thought desperately. *They've got to believe me, and send help!*

Andrew kicked *Dusty's* ribs lightly, and the stallion broke into a fast trot. Then Andrew saw the wagon turning at Bruton Parish Church and head in the direction of the Governor's Palace.

They're going toward the Palace! he thought to himself. *But why? There may be Patriot militia there!*

As he trotted *Dusty* past James Geddy's house he pulled his father's double-barreled pistol from its holster. That's when he saw the carriage standing beside the church wall.

"That's their plan!" he said aloud to *Dusty*. "They're going to put her in that faster carriage and take her out of town in that!"

Ahead of him, Stephen and John and the wagon driver were elated to spy the carriage waiting for them at the side of the road by Bruton Parish Church.

"There's the carriage!" Stephen said. "We made it! Pull the wagon under those trees!"

As the wagon drew closer, two men stepped from beside the carriage. "Got her?" one asked gruffly.

"We sure do!" Stephen replied. He stooped, picked up Sarah still wrapped in the blanket, then stepped onto the wagon seat, and jumped to the ground. Now the two men could see the blindfolded girl, wrapped like a cocoon in the blanket, struggling against the bonds that held her hands and feet. Stephen walked quickly toward the carriage as one of the men opened its door.

"Take that wagon out of town!" Stephen called to the driver. "Then stay away for the next week! No one saw you, I'm sure."

"Yes, sir," the driver said, clucking to the horses as he slapped their backs with the reins.

The sound of pounding hooves startled them all. Out of the night Andrew's stallion burst into the group of men, knocking John against the brick wall, and throwing senseless to the ground one of the carriage drivers. The other carriage driver pulled a long pistol from his belt and aimed it at the horseman. But Andrew's pistol flamed and the man spun with a cry, dropping his weapon as he fell to the ground.

Whirling *Dusty*, Andrew charged toward Stephen, who had just stood Sarah against the side of the carriage. Frightened, Stephen dodged to the side as Andrew leaped from the saddle, his pistol in his hand.

But John leaped back with surprising speed, lunged at Andrew, and grabbed the double-barreled pistol with both his hands. The gun went off as John wrestled it from Andrew's grip.

Andrew slammed his left fist into John's face, then hit his jaw with his right. John grunted with pain, and fell to the ground, the empty pistol falling from his hand.

Stephen, realizing Andrew was now disarmed, stepped toward him, a wicked and triumphant smile barely discernable in the light of the carriage's lantern.

"Your gun's gone, Rebel!" he said. "Show what you can do with your fists!"

He moved swiftly forward and threw a lightening-fast left jab.

Andrew dodged instinctively, but the blow was fast, and stunned him on the side of the head. He stepped back quickly as Stephen moved in again with another left jab.

Again Andrew dodged his head to the side, but again the blow was swift, grazing his skull and stunning him again.

I can't out-box him! Andrew realized in a flash. He recognized Stephen's skill, and knew him to be one of the best boxers in the town. So as Stephen stepped toward him again with another blazing left jab, Andrew used a trick the Indians had taught him. He leaned quickly backwards beyond reach of the punch, pivoted on the ball of his right foot, and swept his left foot against Stephen's lower leg with all his might, knocking it from under him, and knocking the bigger man off balance.

As Stephen staggered, his guard down, Andrew stepped in with a left jab of his own that rocked Stephen's head, then hit him again with a crossing right fist.

With a cry of surprise and rage, the big man stumbled backwards. Andrew followed quickly—but ran into another left to his head, and was stopped.

Limping painfully, Stephen nevertheless stepped in with marvelous balance and threw a right cross at Andrew's head. Andrew barely ducked under the punch as he drove his own right into Stephen's stomach. He followed with a vicious left hook to the ribs.

Again Stephen grunted with pain, but he clubbed Andrew with his left fist as he staggered back to regain his balance.

I can't let him get set! Andrew thought bleakly. He ducked to the side to avoid another left jab, this time slamming the knuckles of his own left fist into the thick muscle of Stephen's arm.

Stephen cried out with pain as his arm went temporarily numb. Andrew stepped in quickly, ducked a roundhouse blow from the big man's right, and slammed two short powerful blows into Stephen's middle.

Stephen gasped, dropping his guard as he leaned forward gulping for breath. This was Andrew's chance, and he didn't waste a moment. His right fist crushed the man's nose against his face. His left caught Stephen's open jaw and slammed it sideways. His right fist caught the falling man on the temple as the big boxer crashed to the ground. Stephen Bancroft lay still.

Chest heaving, Andrew gasped for breath, swaying for a moment, then turned and rushed toward Sarah. The girl was still propped precariously against the carriage, hands and feet tightly bound, although the blanket had by now fallen from around her shoulders. Andrew ripped the blindfold off her face. Then he found the rough knot in the cloth of the gag, and took this off.

He stared at the ropes that bound her, then realized that his knife was in his pack on the horse. The stallion had fidgeted nervously as the men fought, but nevertheless had not run away. Andrew stepped carefully toward him, speaking soothingly. Grabbing the reins, he reached into the pack behind the saddle and removed the belt with his tomahawk and long knife. He also pulled out the rifle from its scabbard and slung it by its strap over his shoulder. Then he dropped the reins and stepped back to Sarah, drew the knife from its sheath, and cut away the ropes that bound her hands and feet.

"Oh, Andrew!" she cried, busting into tears! "I thought I'd never see you again!" She stumbled into his arms, and he held her a moment, his heart filled with black wrath against the men who'd abducted and terrified her.

"Quick!" he said. "We'll ride home!" He turned toward *Dusty*, but Sarah stumbled as she tried to follow him, and fell down.

"Oh, Andrew, my ankles hurt from those ropes!"

"Hold on," he said reassuringly, stooping quickly. She put her arms around his neck as he swept her up and turned again to the stallion.

Suddenly they heard the sound of rushing feet racing toward them.

"They're still there!" a voice shouted in the night, as a group of men ran toward the corner of the church.

"That's the driver of the wagon!" Sarah said, recognizing at once the voice of the man she'd heard on that dreadful trip from the Anthony's home.

Snorting with alarm at the sudden yell and the sound of men running toward them, *Dusty* bolted, and galloped away in the direction of the Governor's Palace!

Andrew was stunned: they were afoot! Sarah couldn't run! They were about to be captured!

CHAPTER THIRTEEN

Flight into Darkness

Andrew whirled with Sarah in his arms, and ran into the darkness as a gang of men raced around the corner of the church and halted in confusion in the darkness.

"There they go on that horse!" one man yelled.

"Quiet!" another snapped. "We've got to be quiet! We can't bring out the town! Someone's already fired a pistol!"

"Don't worry about those shots!" another said quickly. "The stupid militiamen are firing their guns all the time. But I didn't see any riders on that horse!"

"Neither did I!" a fourth man agreed. "When he galloped under that street lantern, I thought the saddle was empty."

"Hey, look at these men on the ground!" one said in shock. "How many men attacked our crew?"

"No way of knowing," the wagon driver said. "But we've got to follow them and get that girl back. She heard me and Stephen and John talking about taking her to the Governor's ship! If she gets away, we'll all be hung!"

"But we can't leave Stephen and these men here—the Rebels will find them!"

"We'll get 'em later," a decisive voice decided. "First, we've got to get back that girl!"

"Listen!" one man said. "I hear someone running!"

Silenced, the men listened.

One of them cursed the faint light from the new moon. "I can't see anything!" he complained.

"Listen!" the man hissed again.

"You're right!" the wagon driver said quickly. "Someone's running through the church yard! I think I see him!"

"How many?" one asked.

"I just saw one!"

"Look!" the wagon driver said. "I saw him between those trees! He's carrying someone, and he's not going fast! Looks like he's heading for the opposite corner of the block, where Nassau crosses Prince George!"

"He must be carrying that girl!" another said quickly. "Let's go! He can't get away from us if he's totin' her! But you stay here, Zach, and try to get Stephen and these two men into the carriage. They've got to get out of here before the militia are alerted and come capture 'em. Then we'd all be caught!"

The remaining men dashed after the faint figure the wagon driver had barely seen by the dim light of the new moon.

"Spread out! He can't get away from four of us!"

Some distance away from the pursuing men, Andrew slowed to a rapid walk. He was behind Mr. George Wythe's house now. He traveled carefully through the darkness, watching for fences, putting the trees between him and the men at the carriage as often as he could, praying that they wouldn't see him. Clearly, he couldn't run for long carrying Sarah; he'd have to alternate running with walking.

He wanted to cross Nassau and head back toward the College as soon as he could, where he'd be more likely to spot the night watch. *But they'll catch us for sure if Sarah can't run!* he thought bleakly.

"Andrew," she said, as if she'd read his mind, "please put me down. I'll try to walk again!"

"Think you can?" he asked, slowing.

"I'll try," she said.

He stopped, and gently let her stand, holding her in his arms a moment as she tested her feet.

"Oh, they hurt, Andrew," she said, " but I know I can walk."

He released her, but took her hand. "Let's go, then."

Slowly she limped beside him, gaining strength as her circulation improved.

But Andrew heard the sound of boots running across the ground of the churchyard behind them.

"They're coming after us!" he said. "Can you run?"

"I'll try," she said. "Hold my hand!"

Slowly she ran; then, as the blood flowed freely into her feet, she ran faster. Andrew's left hand gripped her hand, his right held the long rifle. In a moment he knew that he might have to stop and shoot—if the men came close enough to be seen. *But then they'd rush me and capture her again!* he real-

ized. He could only fire once before the other men would be on
him.

"It's getting better, Andrew!" she said hopefully. "I can
run!"

"Fine!" he replied, scanning desperately the blackness
ahead, praying he'd not lead them straight into a low branch or
tree trunk that would knock them off their feet.

The men behind were closer now, calling to each other in
the darkness.

"Box 'em in!" one called.

"Spread out, then, so they can't go 'round us!" another replied.

Andrew realized their peril. "We've got to turn away from
the way they're headed," he whispered suddenly. "Quick,
we'll go left!"

They turned, swerved suddenly around a large tree, and
stumbled through a cluster of bushes.

"Bend low," he whispered, "those bushes might hide us!"

Suddenly Sarah stumbled. Andrew held her up quickly with
his strong grip. Rapidly they moved across the path of the on-
coming men, praying that their pursuers wouldn't see them
behind the thick bushes and trees.

"I'm all right now," she whispered.

"Thank the Lord for that!" he whispered back. "I think
they've lost us! There's so little light here, and I think they've
gone past us. "Let's go slow, now—we don't want to make
noise. And let's go back toward the College. They may sus-

pect we'd go in the other direction, back toward the Palace, to get *Dusty*."

Again Andrew changed their course, swerving toward the direction of the College. Then he slowed them to a walk to conserve their breath.

"Where's the night watchman?" Sarah whispered, as they walked as fast as they could through the thick bushes which kept catching at her skirts.

"Maybe at the College," he whispered back. "I hope we'll find someone where the roads meet. There's *got* to be someone there!"

They skirted a long picket fence, behind which were the dim outlines of outbuildings. Andrew stopped suddenly, pulling her to a halt with him. He listened intently—but heard no sound of pursuit.

"I think we've gotten away from 'em, Sarah!" He squeezed her hand.

She squeezed his in return.

"I don't hear anyone now," she whispered.

"Neither do I," he replied. "But let's be careful still. We don't know that one of them's not following us and keeping quiet!"

He glanced behind repeatedly as they fled, but could see little through the trees. How thankful he was for the faintness of the moonlight, and for the clouds that sometimes blocked even that light entirely! Those were the only reasons, he realized, that their pursuers hadn't seen them well enough to stay on their trail.

Behind them, the four men in loose skirmish line had come to a confused halt. The wagon driver had crashed into a tree trunk, smashed his face, and fallen to the ground with an outraged cry. The others turned toward him with a rush, thinking that he'd caught their prey. But one man fell face-first into a gully he couldn't see in the dark. He too yelled in rage and pain, and the other two men had stopped in confusion, not knowing which cry to follow.

They called out to each other in anger and perplexity. Finally the men came together.

"They've got away!" the wagon driver said bitterly, holding a large handkerchief to his bleeding face.

The others swore in rage.

"Then we'd better get out of town as fast as we can!" one said, "because when they reach the night watchman he'll turn out all the militia and they'll catch us sure!"

"I'm not going back to the church!" one said. "Who knows if Zach got Stephen and those others out of there! And if he didn't, someone's bound to've found them by now. The place could be crawling with militia!"

"I never thought of that!" another man agreed.

"Let's scatter," the wagon driver said.

With bitter curses the men did just that.

They were wise to have done so.

For Lindsey was trotting *Belle* down Duke of Gloucester Street, accompanied by a dozen outraged armed men trotting beside and behind her.

The men had boiled out of Greenhow's Store and followed her as soon as she's poured out her story. The first man she saw was the one who'd opened the door to her frantic knocking. He listened to her tale, turned instantly, and shouted to a group of men inside. They'd gathered at once—then one of them had recognized Lindsey.

"Miss Lindsey! What are you doing here at this hour? It's dark!"

"Oh, Mr. Jenkins," she cried, overwhelmed with emotion that she'd found someone she knew, "an awful thing has happened!"

Quickly she told of Sarah's capture, and of how Mary and Laurie and she had strung out in the street, following the wagon, until they'd met Andrew.

"But he's gone after them alone, Mr. Jenkins!" she cried out. "Please go help him before he gets hurt! And bring back Sarah!"

Lindsey learned later that there'd been a meeting going on when she'd come to the door. This explained why there were so many armed men present. Now, the outraged citizens acted at once.

"Grab your weapons!" Mr. Jenkins said. "We've got to rescue those two youngsters from the Tories!"

At once the men grabbed their rifles and muskets and rushed out the door.

"Just lead us there, Miss Lindsey," Mr. Jenkins said, as they hurried into the street. "Then you back off. We'll free your friends and escort you home!"

"Yes, Sir," she replied, as one of the men formed a stirrup with his hands and helped her up into the side saddle. Mounted, she whirled *Belle* and headed down the street toward the College.

The men spread out to either side and behind her, running rapidly to keep up with *Belle's* fast trot. The street was quite dark now, and the moon was often behind the clouds. Only the occasional lanterns beside the road, and the lighted windows of the houses they passed, shed light on their way.

"You're a brave girl, Miss Lindsey!" Mr. Jenkins said, as he trotted beside her, long rifle in hand. "So are your young sisters, to follow that wagon like they did! Do you know the men who captured Sarah?"

Before Lindsey could answer, one of the men ahead cried out, "There's a carriage standing by the church!"

At once the crowd of men veered to their right, and raced toward the carriage.

"Pull back, Miss Lindsey," Mr. Jenkins called, "and wait for us here!"

The men fanned out as they ran toward the carriage. As the moon came out from behind the clouds, Lindsey saw two men beside the vehicle. *They're helping someone get in the carriage!* she realized.

Zach had roused one of the men knocked to the ground by Andrew's stallion, and the two of them were struggling to help the dazed Stephen Bancroft into the carriage. But at the sound of the crowd rushing toward them, the two dropped their wounded friend and tried to escape. They were too late. Quickly the Patriots surrounded them, knocking them to the ground, shouting questions, demanding to know the where-abouts of the girl they'd kidnaped.

Lindsey couldn't bear not knowing where Sarah was! In spite of Mr. Jenkins' warning to stay back, she trotted *Belle* closer to the crowd of angry men to see what she could learn. As she approached, the moon came out again, and she saw in its faint light the dim figure of another man lying quite still on the ground. Then she gasped as she recognized the big man who'd been hauled to his feet and propped against the side of the carriage by the angry Patriots.

"Why, that's Stephen Bancroft!" she called out involuntarily.

"Where's the girl you stole?" one of the Patriots shouted to their groggy prisoner, slamming Stephen's head back against the carriage.

Stephen tried to reply. Lindsey couldn't hear his mumbled words, but she did see the sudden blow the big man received when he didn't answer. Stephen collapsed to the ground, but was hauled instantly to his feet.

"He can't talk!" a man shouted, "his jaw's broke! Ask the other one!"

A jumble of voices obscured the man's reply. Anxiously, Lindsey rode *Belle* closer. Then one of the Patriots explained: "He says the girl and the boy got away through the church yard. His friends went after them! He hasn't seen anyone since!"

Quickly the men conferred. Then Mr. Jenkins ran back to Lindsey.

"Andrew got here just in time, Lindsey—thanks to you and your sisters! He shot a man before they could put Sarah into the carriage, and knocked a couple of 'em down with his horse. Then he beat up Stephen—how, we don't know—Stephen's one of the best boxers in town! But that's what this man told us."

"But where are Sarah and Andrew now?" she asked fearfully.

"They got away, the man said. Sarah couldn't walk well, 'cause she'd been tied, and Andrew carried her away through the church yard. This man's friends ran after them. We're sending eight men after them through the yard, while the rest of us run toward the College and sound the alarm. If Sarah can't run, those men will catch 'em for sure!"

As if to confirm his words, three of the men discharged their muskets into the night and began to call, "To arms! To arms!"

Belle neighed in fright, reared, and might have bolted had not Mr. Jenkins grabbed her reins with an iron grip. In a moment the horse settled down.

"Can you ride behind us so's we can escort you home when we rescue Sarah and Andrew?" Mr. Jenkins continued. "I couldn't face your mother and father if I let you ride home by yourself in the night!"

"Yes, Sir," Lindsey said breathlessly, frightened at the near fall from the terrified horse, "I'll ride with you. I want to see Sarah and Andrew safe!" But *Belle*, still skittish, pranced nervously, and it was all Lindsey could do to hold her in check.

"Brave Girl!" Mr. Jenkins said. "You and your sisters have earned the town's gratitude this night, Miss Lindsey!"

"Let's go!" a man shouted. Mr. Jenkins joined the three men who began running in a measured trot toward the College. Windows and doors were flying open and men were calling out, seeking to learn the reason for the three shots and the shouts.

A group of men ran toward them, learned the news, then scattered to spread the alarm. Soon a growing crowd of men was with Mr. Jenkins and his three companions, surrounding *Belle* as they moved rapidly westward on the broad street. Lanterns appeared, seeming to Lindsey as if they floated in air. As they came closer, however, it was clear that they were in the hands of running men—armed men, men with long rifles and long muskets in their hands.

Oh Lord, she prayed, *please let Sarah and Andrew escape! Please let these men find them!*

The moon went suddenly behind the clouds. Lindsey pulled in the reins at once, fearful lest *Belle* trample on one of the men in the crowd that surrounded them.

How will they ever find Sarah and Andrew in this darkness? she asked herself fearfully.

CHAPTER FOURTEEN

They're Patriots!

Andrew and Sarah groped their way in the darkness, past several out-buildings, past a fenced garden, then stepped to the edge of Duke of Gloucester Street, still a block east of the College. Andrew looked carefully toward the College, but saw no sign of the night watch. Suddenly he and Sarah were startled by the sounds of muskets firing! Then they heard men running toward them.

"Back!" Andrew said, pulling her with him into the shadow of a large tree. He released her hand, unslung his long rifle from his back, and cocked the weapon.

Oh, Lord! he prayed. *I'll just have one shot before they're on us! Don't let them be Bancroft's men!*

But would Bancroft's men be making that much noise, attracting attention to themselves like this?

"Who could they be?" Sarah whispered anxiously.

"Well, I'm not sure. . ." he said, still uncertain. Then he heard one of the approaching men yell for the night watch. And he saw other men running behind them, also heading toward the College.

"Mr. Bancroft's men wouldn't be calling the night watch!" he said excitedly. "They tried to keep quiet when they were stealing you away! I think they're Patriots!"

"Oh, Andrew, do you think so?" she said, stepping close behind him and peering around his shoulder.

"I sure do!" he said, lowering the barrel of his rifle. "C'mon! We've found friends!"

And find friends they did! For as the men came closer, and passed under the light of a lantern, they each recognized Mr. Jenkins.

"That's *Belle* behind them!" Sarah cried out in surprise. "And Lindsey! I recognize her dress!"

"Mr. Jenkins!" Andrew called, as the men came closer.

At once Sarah and Andrew were surrounded by a joyful group of men, with Lindsey on *Belle* right behind them.

"Sarah!" Mr. Jenkins said, "are we glad we found you!"

"So am I! Mr. Jenkins," the grateful girl replied.

"Sarah!" Lindsey cried out.

"Oh, Lindsey, did you lead these men here?"

"She certainly did!" Mr. Jenkins answered. "She and her sisters followed the wagon that took you away. Then they met Andrew. And Lindsey and Andrew followed you to the store. While Andrew kept following you and the wagon, Lindsey ran in and told us what had happened. But we thought those men had taken you away!"

"They would have, if Andrew hadn't ridden into them and stopped them!" she said. "They were putting me in that carriage. They were going to take me to the Governor's ship as a spy!"

Lindsey jumped down and hugged her friend as Mr. Jenkins questioned Andrew. Then, they all turned quickly as a group of mounted men galloped up and pulled to a stop, the horses snorting nervously and prancing.

"That's Mr. Anthony!" Sarah cried in delight.

"Father!" Lindsey cried, as she ran to him. He leaped from his horse and swept her into his arms.

"Mary and Laurie roused the neighbors," Anthony told them, "and I got home just as they were ready to follow Lindsey back into the darkness! Thank God you're safe, Sarah!"

"Oh, Mr. Anthony, if Lindsey and Mary and Laurie hadn't followed the wagon, no one would have known where those men were taking me! Then Andrew couldn't have stopped them, and I'd be on the way to the Governor's ship!" She burst into tears.

Holding Lindsey with one arm, Anthony reached out the other and hugged Sarah. "Thank God that they did follow you, Sarah, and thank God that Andrew did stop those men! You're safe now! Let's get you home!"

"We've got your horse, Andrew," Mr. Jenkins said, as one of the men rode up leading *Dusty*. "We found him wandering on Duke of Gloucester and hoped we'd find you so you could ride him home!"

"Let's take these girls home!" Anthony said decisively, as he mounted his horse and pulled Lindsey up with him. The group turned and headed back along Duke of Gloucester Street. Sarah rode *Belle*, Mr. Anthony rode with Lindsey in his arms, and Andrew rode *Dusty*.

The men on horseback clustered around Andrew, plying him with questions about his fight with Stephen and his gang. He told them of shooting one of the men, of dismounting and striking another, and then of his fight with Stephen.

"Stephen's one of the best boxers in the town, Andrew," one of the men said in genuine puzzlement. "I've seen him beat good boxers into the ground on Public Days. How'd you whip him?"

"Not by boxing alone," Andrew replied. "He's too good — better'n I am! But I used my feet, like my Indian friends taught me, and I kicked his leg out from under him once as he was punching me. Then I got some good licks in. But he was the fastest I'd ever seen! Even when I ducked, his fist caught my head!"

"How'd you put him away, then?" another man asked.

Andrew tried to remember the sequence of the fight and describe it to his eager hearers. The group passed Greenhow's store. Then they came to the next street. Here Anthony pulled his horse to a halt. "I'll take Lindsey home," he said. "Want to come along so's I can ride back with you, or do you feel safe enough now to go by yourselves?" he asked Andrew and Sarah.

"We're fine now, Mr. Anthony," Andrew said firmly. "That gang's scattered and some of 'em are captured. And those that got away—the ones chasing us—are on foot! They can't reach us now. We'll ride right home—Sarah's parents will be frantic until they see her! I'll take her right home."

"I may meet her father coming from my house," Anthony replied. "That's where Sarah was supposed to be returning from. If I see him, I'll tell him you two are on the way. "Good night, then," Anthony said with a wave.

"Oh, Lindsey!" Sarah exclaimed as they parted, "How can I ever thank you—and Mary and Laurie?"

"It's thanks enough and plenty to have you safe, Sarah!" Lindsey replied. "My family will be so happy to hear that you're rescued!"

"God bless you, Lindsey!" Andrew said quietly. "You're a brave girl!"

Anthony rode off with Lindsey in his arms. Andrew and Sarah continued down Duke of Gloucester Street before turning right toward their part of town. And in fact, before they reached home, their fathers and two other armed men galloped up behind them.

"We just left the Anthonys!" Mr. Edwards said as he pulled his horse to a walk beside *Belle*. "He told us what happened! We knew something was wrong when you didn't return, Sarah, so we rode out looking for you."

Again Andrew and Sarah went through their story, telling of her capture, of the Anthony girls' following her in the darkness, of Lindsey's gathering the men from a meeting at the tavern, and of Andrew's fight at the church. Both Andrew and Sarah were near exhaustion now, and desperately anxious to get home.

When they reached her house, Sarah's father took *Belle's* reins. "Go on in, Sarah," he said. "Your mother will be mighty glad to see you!"

She climbed wearily from the saddle, then looked up toward Andrew. He'd pulled *Dusty* to a halt. But she couldn't think of anything to say. Not even a word!

She couldn't see his smile in the darkness. "Bye!" he said, as he kicked *Dusty* into motion. "See you in the morning."

"Bye," she said finally.

Then he was gone. She wiped her sleeves across her eyes and stumbled up the steps. The door flew open, and she fell into her mother's arms.

Nelson Edwards held *Belle's* reins in his hand as he watched his daughter disappear into the house. Then he turned to Andrew, who was abreast his own house now. "Thanks, Andrew!" he called.

"Yes, Sir," Andrew replied, turning in the saddle. "I'm just thankful the Anthony girls led me to Sarah!"

"I am too, Andrew! And I'm thankful also that you attacked Bancroft and his men and rescued her." Edwards paused, but couldn't think of any way to say what was in his heart. Andrew waited politely while the older man groped for words. Finally, Edwards said simply, "Good night, Andrew."

"Good night, Sir," Andrew replied.

Then he turned *Dusty* again toward home. Andrew barely remembered taking the horse to the barn, unsaddling and rubbing him down, and giving him food and water.

Finally he stumbled wearily toward the house, his long rifle in his hand.

At the other end of town, shortly after Andrew and Sarah had reached their homes, the angry Patriots captured two of the four men who'd chased Andrew and Sarah into the darkness. They handled their prisoners roughly. Terrified, the captured men quickly told of Stephen Bancroft's role in the kidnaping, and of the plan to take Sarah to the Governor's ship as a spy. Further, they told how Stephen's father was behind the plot.

"I thought so!" Mr. Jenkins said grimly. "I never believed he was sincere when he said he'd give no more help to Governor Dunmore! Tom, take some men and bring Bancroft to the Tavern. We'll all gather there."

Tom called out for five men to follow him, then led them at a fast trot to the Bancroft home. Here he sent two men to cover the back, while he with the rest went up on the porch and began slamming the brass knocker against the door.

In a few moments, the light of a lantern flickered against the panes of glass above the door. Then a frightened servant opened the door and in a quavering voice asked the men what they wanted.

"Where's Mr. Bancroft?" Tom called. His friends crowded around him, their long muskets pointed at the man in the door.

"He's gone!" the terrified servant replied. "He's taken everyone but Mr. Stephen with him. They're all gone to join the Governor! There's only two of us here now, me and my wife!"

But Tom insisted on searching the house. The frightened servant led them through every room, and they could see that he had been telling the truth: Mr. Bancroft had gone indeed.

Tom gathered the men in the back yard, and led them all back toward Greenhow's Tavern to report.

Here a group of Patriots had collected to discuss the events of the night. Extra men were put on watch. The captains of the militia companies were told to be aware of escaped Tories. And plans were made to make the town more secure for its citizens.

"This is outrageous!" Mr. Jenkins said, "that a girl was actually kidnaped from in front of one of our homes! We can't let this happen again!"

"We've got to watch those who sympathize with the Governor and the King," another said grimly, "and see that they can't serve Dunmore's orders any longer—not while they live in this town!"

Gradually, the militiamen returned to their homes. The lights began to go out in the windows. Soon the town was asleep.

CHAPTER FIFTEEN

There's No Turning Back!

The fire crackled merrily in the crowded room of the Raleigh Tavern and warmed the men who'd come in from the cold December air. Half-a-dozen of them had pulled up chairs around the corner booth where Captain Innes and Mr. George Wythe were questioning Andrew Hendricks. Most were drinking hot cider, but some drank hot chocolate, or coffee. William Hendricks sat beside his son in the booth, smoking his clay pipe, as his son described the battle at Great Bridge. The assembled men hung on his every word.

Andrew gave a gripping account of the battle, then answered a barrage of questions from the eager listeners. He then told them of Governor Dunmore's now-precarious military position.

"Colonel Woodward thinks Dunmore's force is broken," he concluded. "And he's taking the Second Regiment closer to Norfolk. He believes he can take the town from the British now."

There was a stir among the men at this prospect. This was the most hopeful news they'd had of Virginia's military situation for several months. Norfolk in British hands was a powerful thorn in Virginia's side, and a serious threat to all the settlements and shipping of the Chesapeake Bay. George Wythe was the first to speak.

"So the colonel thinks that Dummore's lost that much power by this battle, Andrew?" he asked thoughtfully. "As battles go, it was not a large one."

"Yes, Sir, he does. Because the Second Regiment and the North Carolina militia have cut off Norfolk from its food supplies in those nearby counties. And it was a British unit, their professional soldiers, that was beaten in the field by our militia. So he thinks that will discourage the Virginians who went over to Governor Dunmore's side when he was winning all the fights."

"The colonel has a good point," Captain Innes said. "Norfolk can't support a large force without food from the inland counties. And if the Second Regiment and the North Carolinians beat the British regular troops, the Virginians who defected to the King will have to think twice before taking the field again. Small as the fight was, if it broke Dunmore's hold on eastern Virginia, it's as big a victory as we could need—or pray for!"

The other men murmured assent. "This is the first real defeat for Dunmore and the British in our area," one of them said. "And it may be decisive; at least it could give us time to train our militia."

"Strange, how a small event can have such huge consequences in a large war!" a man commented.

"The work of every single individual who does his duty can be decisive in ways that we'll never know," Captain Innes said.

William Hendricks spoke then. "If this victory at Great Bridge has given Virginia a respite, we've got to use the time well. We've got to use every hour we have to prepare our militia to face British troops in battle."

"You're right, William," said George Wythe. "And I know our military leaders know that."

"But they've got to get the militia units the proper supplies, Mr. Wythe!" Andrew volunteered. "You'd be shocked if you'd seen how short they were of powder, and of blankets, and flour! That was our biggest problem—it was our lack of supplies!"

"That's going to be the key to all our efforts," another man said reflectively. "Whether or not we'll be vigorous in supplying the men we put in the field. In all our wars with France and with their Indian allies, we've never faced a task of this magnitude."

George Wythe picked up on Andrew's comment. "Well, from what Andrew tells us, we haven't done a good job of keeping one regiment properly supplied—not even for a couple of months. If we don't learn to do better, it bodes ill for our future success in fighting the British Empire."

No one present realized at the time that they'd touched on the one problem that was to come so close to defeating the entire American effort to win their independence from Great Britain.

Then the men discussed the latest news from the north. "We've sent some regiments to take Canada from the British," George Wythe said.

"Canada?" a man asked. "But the British have troops there!"

"Not many, our messengers tell us. And the French hate England, as we all know."

"But we're English too, we Americans," a man said decisively. "And the French in Canada hate us as much as they hate England!"

"That's a good point," George Wythe said. "But our leaders in Congress think that the Canadians would rather be our neutral allies than England's captives."

"That's a desperate gamble!" Captain Innes said. "But if France thinks we're trying to free their citizens from England, they might send over their fleet to help us!"

"That's what our leaders hope," Wythe replied. "They hope France will help us in our war with England. In fact, Patrick Henry's urged our House of Burgesses, and the Continental Congress as well, to send representatives to France, and Spain, and Portugal, and ask them for financial and military aid. All those nations have been humbled by Great Britain in recent wars. Henry thinks that this chance to get their revenge on England will ensure the success of our own resistance as well. We need their aid, in fact."

An hour later, Andrew and his father put their horses in the barn and walked toward the house. "That was a good account you gave, Andrew," William Hendricks said reflectively. "It helped us all to hear about the fight from a man who was actually there."

Then he clapped his son's shoulder and grinned. "I don't have to tell you that once the rumors start arriving, there'll be a score of different versions of the battle circulating around Williamsburg!"

They stepped up the steps of the back porch, and William Hendricks opened the door to go in, when they were stopped by a voice from the Edwards house next door.

"Andrew!" Sarah called. "Can you come here a minute?"

William Hendricks grinned at Andrew. "Go on, Son. You saved her from being a British captive last night! You know she wants to thank you." He grinned and gripped Andrew's shoulder again. Then he went inside.

Andrew's face grew red. He turned, stepped off the porch, and walked toward the Edwards home. Sarah stood on the porch at the top of the steps and waited for him. He walked up and stopped at the bottom of the steps.

"Goodness, Sarah, where's your coat?"

She stood before him in her dark brown dress, and at first didn't know what to say. *How can I possibly thank him for what he did last night to rescue me?* she asked herself.

Then she realized that she'd been looking at him for a long moment without saying a word. She blushed suddenly, turned, and hurried toward the door. "C'mon," she said. "I baked a pie!"

Andrew grinned, and ran up the steps after her. "Sure," he said, as he followed her inside. "I don't mind that! Long as your father's not around to accuse me of stealing *his* pie!"

She laughed. The embarrassment between them was broken now. "Oh, don't worry. He's gone to the printing office. Besides, I made him another one."

Andrew followed her inside.

The Battle at Great Bridge

December 11, 1775

At Great Bridge in Virginia, just South of Norfolk Town,
The British built a sturdy Fort, and sent their Redcoats
  down.
They planned to strike before the Patriot Units could unite;
To crush the Rebel Companies piecemeal, and put to Flight
The battered scattered Remnants, who'd spread Panic in
  their Path
To Safety; As the Tribes out West began their great Blood-
  bath
Against the Patriot Settlements, until, from East to West
Virginia's Rebel Forces—shattered—crumbled in the
  Dust...

Virginia's Second Regiment set out in desperate Haste
From Williamsburg to Suffolk, where Dunmore's Troops
  had chased
Away Virginia's Forces. Now, facing Dunmore's Fort,
The Regiment stood guard for Weeks, awaiting Arms and
  Shot
And Cannon to defend themselves when Dunmore's Men
  should charge;
And Blankets to ward off the Cold, and Men, who would
  enlarge
Their Numbers to withstand the Foe when British troops
  would come
Against their Ranks, with Bayonets and smoking blazing
  Guns.
The British charged! The Redcoats came! With naked steel
  out thrust,

With Volleys fierce of Musketry to bring down to the Dust
Militiamen who formed in Ranks and waited for the Call
To fire their Rifles at the Foe.—And tho' the Fight was
  Small
By later Battle-Standards, Yet the Issue here was great!
For if the Patriots faltered now, and if they fled their Fate,
If they gave way to Fear and Flight, if they fell back, and
broke,
Virginia's Freedoms might collapse, might crumble at the
  Stroke
Of Murray, Earl of Dunmore, the Victorious Governor
Who'd never given up the fight, who'd sworn to persevere
For England's King and Parliament and for their hated
  Sway,
Their Rule above all Law and Right.—'Twas a Momentous
  Day!

The Fight was small—but Pivotal! For if Virginia lost
This Battle, then her units would be driven from her Coast;
The vast Supplies she sent up North to help those Patriots
  fight
Would stop at once! Her troops would have to hasten back
  in fright;
The Colonies' united Power would wither on the Vine,
Virginia Herself would surely—helpless—lay supine
Before Lord Dunmore's Troops and Tribes, and well might
  fall and fail,—
Enslaved, impoverished, ravished, bound beneath the Ty-
  rant's Heel.
The Redcoats fired and charged—but then their yelling
  Ranks were downed

By Patriot Volleys! Men collapsed, their Charge thus
  quickly ground
To fatal hesitation—and then to fearful Flight!
Virginia's Second Regiment had wrecked the Tyrants
  Might!